AVIARIES

Zuzana Brabcová

AVIARIES

Translated from the Czech by
Tereza Novická

TWISTED SPOON PRESS

PRAGUE

2019

ISBN 978-80-86264-51-6

This translation was made possible by a grant
from the Ministry of Culture of the Czech Republic.

MINISTERSTVO
KULTURY

For Richie

The day is a chest with a false bottom.
Richard Weiner

December 20, 2011

It arrives around four, five o'clock in the afternoon, hangs around until about seven, and then at night, it reigns. It's been that way for years, I don't recall it ever having been any different. A day devoted to staying in is the music of a melody nobody has ever played. And when I do have to go out, there's a bloom coating the people I pass, a frost blurring their features. I can imagine they don't exist, and in this way love them. All that exists: just disrupts and mars, as if somebody had graffiti-tagged *The Night Watch*.

Václav Havel died the day before yesterday. In his sleep, in the morning. So its reign extends beyond night.

December 21, 2011

"Did I ever cry my heart out, lady! I sure was fond of him!" said the woman at Anděl from whom I sometimes bought the street magazine *Nový prostor*.

It was close to freezing, she had no gloves. It had been close to freezing all day long, all day long she had no gloves, all day long she shuffled back and forth along the tram stop.

"Why aren't you wearing gloves?"

"They're expensive," she replied.

She was missing teeth, too, both uppers and lowers.

They're even more expensive.

I went around the corner to the Christmas market and bought her a pair of gloves. Her face lit up with a rounded emptiness while I recoiled in disgust at my own gesture, and she used the gloves to hungrily squeeze Christmas by the neck.

December 22, 2011

This bloom: not just on people, but on things, too, and between me and them towers a mirror wall set into a rectangular frame. The shop jingles, smelling of frankincense.

I could stand behind the curtain for hours and hours, watching Míra and Bobeš dribbling the ball, a static image in motion, but I don't have a curtain.

I wipe off the dust and look into the dictionary: "Microscopic particles of a substance that is of mineral or organic origin produced by the process of disintegration, accumulating as dirt."

Something is happening. Something's in the air. Something isn't right.

Sometimes

"Hey lady, gimme a cig!"

Sometimes the fear I'll disappear in others like a handful of snow. I give the old Gypsy woman a cig.

"Gimme some money, at least some change, it being Christmas 'n' all!"

I give her fifty crowns.

"And wrinkles, gimme your wrinkles!"

I remove them one by one, the wrinkles from my face, a bundle of used toothpicks. She throws them into her enormous pocket and jumps out of the tram at the last minute.

My face is completely cleared of everything, like dough rolled thin, just position the cookie cutter, apply pressure, and cut out a star.

I enter a pub, on my own for the first time, it's called Hlubina, The Depths. A drunk takes a seat next to me, and his eyes sink into my brain like into a bloody tub full of carp.

"Are you afraid of getting old?" he asks.

We get drunk remarkably quickly and efficiently, and then in front of the pub he urinates onto the tire of a Land Rover smothering the entire street like a gigantic tombstone.

A three-day period of national mourning is declared. At night, within the borders of its domain, I turn on the computer and read what's written in the bubble in the bottom right corner: *Your system may be at risk.* I suddenly hear sentences in my head, they don't belong to me and I have no idea how they got there: "I would like to discover basic ethical concepts through which I could measure my life, I am, however, fascinated by the dark trajectory of thoughts and emotions. I transcend my own being in an unknown direction."

A day of national mourning

I'm coming back home, down the hallway by the basement stalls. I live in the basement. Above my head, the lights turn on automatically, one by one. I suddenly spot a snake edging toward me across the concrete floor. It goes still. I go still. It raises its head, flat and speckled. We watch each other warily, a barely audible hiss from the light bulbs. At that very moment, the wail of the noon siren splits through the hissing and the city freezes in a minute of silence in honor of the deceased. Quiet steps draw closer down the hallway. A man nimbly pins the snake's head to the concrete floor with a forked hook and then lifts it into the air.

"So sorry, I apologize . . . it must've scared you . . . it escaped from my terrarium . . . the door to the hall was open . . ."

Now I know what those strange sporadic thuds coming from upstairs mean. It's my neighbor hitting lab mice against the table to kill them for his snake.

Sometimes

anxiety resembles a cave in which a guide is describing the formation of stalagmites and stalactites in a monotone,

other times

it's close-fitting and skintight.

And during these days

Alice arrived. Her face showed quite different things than when she had left half a year ago, such strikingly rounded things, without edges. I imagined her running with her dogs along the shore where buildings both near and far look like eggs.

She sat down in a wicker armchair, started to roll a cigarette, but immediately sprang up and ran around the room and began to dance and gesticulate, before sitting down again. Her body, suddenly so palpable and concrete, was constantly on the move, in a whirl, circling that abstract statue her mother had turned into these past few months.

"Each morning we have to walk two kilometers to fetch water and back again, and we go to the bathroom in the woods, we dig a hole and then cover it back up . . ."

She was laughing! She was smiling happily thanks to the

stolen scrap of paradise, the illusion where flushers weren't suspended from the stars and the glow of monitors had been crushed by the heel of darkness.

I heard a voice, Alice's voice was drawing nearer to me on a rope like a tightrope walker: "Ninety percent of the wealth of this planet is owned by one percent of the population."

A dust bunny stirred up by her steps rolled up and down the floor, snowballing more and more layers of time.

And during this night

I opened the discussion thread under an article about V.H.

"Hope he's rotting in hell, the old hack."

Something stirred within the depths of the world's grinder and sniggered and heehawed. In the murk of scum, in the silent and holy night, revulsion stirred.

The hairs of the moment bristled,

and it crouched and barked. In the Chamber of Deputies, four Communist MPs refused to honor the memory of the first Czech president, spearheaded by the leader of the Prague Communists, Marta Semelová, who instead congratulated the nation on ridding itself of a pest.

Marta Semelová used to be Alice's first-grade teacher. "Your daughter is extremely gifted, she'll make something of herself one day," she said and covered Alice's head with her palm like a fortune-teller.

Can the prophetic gesture of a Communist even mean anything? A bark, bristled hair, a pointed sneer? No. It meant absolutely nothing.

Alice

enters the forest. She wants to take part in the memorial ceremony for the late president. The forest is deserted though, the
neighing of a Kladruber horse reaches her only from afar — a
distance in time, not space. One minute Alice is bouncing
around in the blueberries, she's two years old, the next she's
barely hobbling along, an old woman she is yet to become — no
chance of pinning down her actual age on this path.

"You're twenty-three!" I yell after her. She can't hear me.
Maybe because the trees around her are growing upside down,
their crowns rooted into the ground, while knotworks of roots
rise skyward. She can't hear me: for that forest is in my belly
and she has not yet been born.

Christmas Eve, 2011

Whenever a celebrity dies, my mom draws a little cross next to
their name in her encyclopedia. "I made a cross!" she announces
from the hallway, and her lips that have been opening and closing for the past eighty-eight years crack into a barely noticeable,
thin shadow of a smile. I can't stand it. I step onto the balcony
and light a cigarette. A woman about my age is standing on the
balcony opposite, lighting a cigarette. It's not clear, both of us
starting to shiver from the cold, which one of us is the reflection
in the mirror and which is standing in front of it. Crisscrossed
splinters, thin Christmas candles and skewers, my mother's
crosses, they all madly fly across the maw of the courtyard from
the woman to me and from me back to her.

I lift a huge, heavy pot full of potato salad from the balcony
floor.

"Death is a mere part of hard life," Mom sighs the line of a poem from her favorite poet and lovingly leafs through one cross after another.

Fingers tearing through wrapping paper, I notice I have brown spots on the backs of my hands that weren't there last year. "Are you afraid of getting old?" The wax weeps, and a light, hollow ball quivers on a hook in a nest of pine needles.

We sit inside that ball at the table: my sister Nadia, her husband, my niece with a newborn baby Jesus in her arms, the baby screaming, a stink overpowering the potpourri, Mom, and Alice.

I still can't believe she's sitting next to me and I can touch her, embrace her. One more carol, one more toast — and then we all tuck into the snake with relish, coiled up neatly on our plates.

And one winter day

is exactly the 428th day I've been out of work. On October 31, 2010, I was laid off for redundancy as per labor code regulations. Officially, it all went down by the book — a two-month notice plus three months of severance pay. I could be the envy of many a wandering ghost at Anděl weighed down by their belongings in plastic bags. I still buy gloves for women selling *Nový prostor*. I still pay the gas bill. I can still pay my way when getting drunk with a stranger.

My friend and boss started to devote all his time to hockey. Just a pair of high-quality Bauer ice skates costs 7,499 crowns. He spent most of his day on the ice. He spent most of his time skating. Either alone or as a chaperone to his sons, transformed into two little golems by their gear. High-end Easton shin guards cost 2,699 crowns, and the ten years spent in each other's company melted away like a lump of butter in the sun, greasily, messily.

Yet since then I've been shepherded by Miss Linda Řádná, who is here for me like a loyal partner in a time of economic misery, a carabiner hammered into the rock of a social crevice, and, sitting in front of the computer, she exposes her fragile profile to me, a clinging profile that seeps into and is absorbed by the light cast from God knows where, the small hard round black light that hits me right between the eyes like a puck.

"Anything new?"

"Unfortunately, no."

But our optimism doesn't flag, neither hers, nor mine, not with a plan of action for job seekers to execute. She prints out three, four job offers for me. I'll take anything. I have three days to bring back confirmation that I'm redundant even for these, otherwise Miss Řádná will strike me from the register.

An usherette. I want to work as an usherette!

Linda lifts her eyes to the ceiling until only two whites remain. In that moment she resembles a Baroque saint in ecstasy, and I might have fallen in love with her just a little.

I'm taken aback when Mr. Herbert Klein informs me that I've been included in the selection process along with another three hundred and twenty-eight applicants. I have to fill out a questionnaire first. The questionnaire for the usherette position is nine pages long. I can't believe my eyes when I get to the twenty-first question, "What do you consider the meaning of your life to be?"

As usual, the hallway of the Prague 5 employment office is crowded and lively as an airport terminal. Waiting number tickets are crumpled in sweaty palms while arrival and departure times flash on the display and promptly disappear. "Anything new?" "Unfortunately, no." The waiting numbers in everyone's hands gradually become hard marbles: I can't shake the idea that the thing to do, right here, right now, in the middle of the hallway, during this one single unrepeatable second of one winter day, would be to hollow out a hole in the grimy linoleum, a deep pit, a crater monstrously agape, a grave, and then fall to our knees and start playing.

January 30, 2012

A party for Mom's eighty-eighth birthday. Close friends and relatives mill about the spacious Smíchov apartment, they come close and move away to other rooms, and while snippets of conversations reach me, I babble at my little grandnephew: "Blam-bu-la, blam-bu-la . . ."

"Rampula should immediately resign from his post . . ."

"Ram-pu-la, ram-pu-la . . ." Post: first, a member of the prison guard; second, an assigned position, employment; third, a vertical support, marker, or structure.

"A direct election for president? You want Landa or Gott to be president?"

"Double, double toil and trouble, fire burn, and cauldron bubble!"

My grandnephew starts to bawl. My sister falls silent and swoops toward him, the others by contrast start to shout to make themselves heard over him.

"They've stolen everything, the bastards, and now the middle class gets the short end of the stick!"

Mom turns to me, "Now don't forget to buy me those cleaning tablets for my dentures."

"He shat himself!" my sister announces triumphantly.

"I better write it down for you."

Alice hands her grandma a pencil. "What kind of weird pencil is this?"

"It's a Versatil," my mother explains with an inexplicable seriousness in her voice, as if she were elucidating the third law of thermodynamics.

"Versa what?"

A Versatil mechanical pencil.

Under the touch of that word, the whole of me shrinks into a ball like a hedgehog, rays of childhood shoot out of me like spines left, right, and center. The fan of arrows then shoots out of my body and soars over the laden table, it whooshes back and forth across the space, above the champagne and platters of food, I drink everything, even Metaxa, which I've never liked.

Rampula, he shat himself, Versatil, Karel Gott, and childhood, my childhood, now duly celebrating via the tenor and clapping its wings, applauding itself, wings so moldered and rotted that lumps and pieces of feathers rain down into the glasses.

Disgusting.

"I know you think it's important now, but you won't even remember it in twenty years."

To whom is my eighty-eight-year-old mother telling this, this wise old woman with the voice of a mischievous schoolgirl? To us all? It makes sense in my grandnephew's case, sure, but . . .

I again find myself leafing through the *Dictionary of Standard Czech*, this time looking for "Versatil." The adjective "versatile" catches my eye: variable, changeable. Med.: children with versatile idiocy.

I glance worriedly at Kryštof: his diaper's been changed and he's calm.

"What is truly irrational and genuinely inexplicable is not evil but, on the contrary, good."

Who said that? I look around at my family members, confused: where did that sentence come from? My sister and niece are bending down toward the toddler drowning in baby rattles, the men are quietly discussing gas mileage, and Alice has slipped off with her cousin to the balcony to smoke a joint.

It may have just erupted out of nowhere or out of some utterly ordinary object — a salt shaker or a mug with coffee grounds, a windowpane or even out of this Versatil, whose sharp nib has injected my vein with that familiar, yet always new, fear: something is happening. Something's in the air. Something isn't right.

I look at the shaky handwriting in front of me — it clearly says: *cleaning tablets for dentures.*

And suddenly, in the jumble of voices and whirl of curtains, in the lumps and pieces of what I used to be long ago and what only old black-and-white photographs remind me of, I can hear my childhood clattering down the slide in the courtyard below.

February 21, 2012

Like spring: timid and craven, as if spring had hesitantly touched the air and then retracted its two feelers in fear. Sunny-like, so I go out, I take a walk, treading a mud-like path through the woods behind the Motol Cemetery, down paths full of dog shit and beer cans and branches from which slimy strands of tallow hang, and I meet a jogger, a fat butt and thighs in leggings, she really could use the exercise, I pass an old man stabbing the mud with his Nordic walking poles, two young ladies, each clutching

a small Pekinese instead of purses, "And so I, like, told him . . ."
— "So he must've been well pissed off like!" the other one
laughs, and on buses and on the subway and in the crowd at the
Anděl intersection, everyone everywhere is weaving "like" into
their speech, as if nothing were genuine anymore, as if every
second extended hundreds of possibilities, countless parallel
options, but none that held true. And it wouldn't even surprise
me now if I were to meet a diver, for instance, a diver floating
along the path behind the Motol Cemetery with a snorkel longer
than the longest antenna, a snorkel looming above the treetops
to the sky, an endless hollow tube penetrating into the cosmos
and curving alongside it, only from there inhaling that which
makes life imaginable, indeed even possible.

I press my cheek to the bark and then bury my face into it.
When I tear it away a moment later, my nose, forehead, and left
cheek stay stuck to the pine tree — I make a futile attempt to
pull it off with my fingernails.

So spring, so the sun, so a tree face till death, good only for
Alice maybe to whittle a boat from.

Divers

With satisfied astonishment, or rather, astonished satisfaction,
I've observed over these past days and weeks that the world has
turned into an enormous interior carved by right angles, yes,
into a maze, a labyrinth, a tangle of rectangular corridors, where
the signs hanging on all the doors read: WAIT TO BE CALLED.

Since the day Alice left to go back to her dumpsters brim-
ming with the excess of a civilization going extinct, I've been
spending most of my time in the waiting rooms of offices and
doctors. I don't knock on the door to announce my presence

but obediently wait to be called, patiently leafing through the magazines. In the waiting room of psychiatrist Radan Gnuj, where everything, the chairs, carpet, even walls are a matching brown-pink prenatal color, I come across the following passage: *The madness of consumerism forces people to keep buying new things while getting rid of the old. So-called dumpster divers collect these discarded items out of trash containers and thereby draw attention to the illogical surplus of our capitalist society. Part of this phenomenon comprises the recycling of food that all supermarket chains dispose of right before its expiration date. Some retailers pour chemicals on the perishables to render them inedible, though it is possible to reach an agreement with some chains (Billa, Albert). And then one is free to plunge into the depths of the dumpster (called diving).*

Mostly I blindly stare at a page with celebrities comparing their cleavages and happen to notice my hands: they're trembling, and there's a space between them like between two stars. In a moment of panic I press both of my palms together, as though I were about to pray, and firmly intertwine my fingers almost to the point of pain to crush that interstellar space between them. "Diving" is on the rise mainly among the elderly here. It was only a few days ago that the government announced its intent to freeze pensions for three years.

"Next!" Startled, I wrench apart my knitted fingers, causing stigmata to appear on my palms.

I find myself no longer sitting in Doctor Gnuj's psychiatric womb, but in a waiting room for an MRI. I draw one gallows after another on the gigantic board that is here for patients to pass the time, simply because I don't know how to draw anything else. An old man with a bandaged neck and both arms in a cast who an orderly wheeled in on a gurney is watching me.

"They're empty," he rasps.

"Sorry?"

"You have to draw the hanged man, too."

"I don't know how to."

"I do . . . but . . ." he grimaces apologetically and abruptly lifts his plastered arms, making the orderly jump.

We're not allowed to wear bracelets and earrings or have pacemakers and dentures. I remember the denture tablets I was supposed to buy Mom.

In a couple of minutes, I'm disappearing into the tunnel.

"Squeeze the balloon if you have a problem."

A mass looms two centimeters above me, a steel slab, a block of granite, a Tertiary boulder, an alloy of anxiety and laughter, what do I know. A headset covering my ears, I rumble and rattle as though the tunnel had started to move with me and was rushing down a much larger tunnel. I'm in an endless complex of tunnels, one sliding into the other like the tubes of a spyglass, in a complex falling steeply downward at the speed of neutrino particles, all the way to the very bottom where a nasty brown clod lies, my past resembling horse shit. My fingers make a feeble attempt to locate the balloon. I'll never be able to do it, even if the entire world contracted into a single tunnel.

2:11 a.m., the night of February 13, 2012

Maybe at this precise hour and minute Alice and Bob Dylan — only his parents are to blame for his name — are lowering themselves to the bottom of a dumpster. They go out at night, so I'm told. It suddenly strikes me: they need a headlamp! A flashlight for the speleological head.

When in the small hours of dawn, birds shrieking and day

breaking, I eventually find myself in a cave, I don't have one: I'm surrounded by pitch-black darkness and the squeaking of bats; stalaglights and stalactights point at me from all directions, aiming at my forehead like rapiers until the earth's hard and damp crust finally speaks:

> *How to brave that moment,*
> *an hour? two? one afternoon?*
> *half a delirious night? — and how to brave*
> *the moment they all leave,*
> *the living, the barely living, the phantoms —*
> *once the children leave,*
> *once the door closes behind them . . .*

And that's why without having brushed my teeth or finished my coffee I set out that very same morning for Hudy Sport on Lidická Street.

The young woman standing behind the counter could easily compete in a most-impressive-celebrity-cleavage contest.

"Can I help you?" The smile that slashes her face like a razor indicates I could ask for anything.

"I'm looking for a headlamp."

She pirouettes from her spot behind the counter and takes me gently, almost imperceptibly, by the elbow and leads me to a huge rack filled top to bottom with an assortment of downright baffling objects.

"As you can see, we have a very wide selection. This, for instance, is the deluxe headlamp LED Lenser H73, it's small, lightweight, and high-performance, and please note its optical specs. A luminosity of 16 lumens with a range of up to 170 meters. Given these specs, the price of 2,250 crowns is practically nothing . . ."

I can feel myself stiffening into a statue. Into a monument of an athlete, alpinist, and speleologist sealed head to toe in Hudy Sport gear.

"But I . . ."

The young lady is already pointing at another mysterious object. "This is the Petzl Tikka 2XP," her voice softens, "the body is tiltable . . ." The body is tiltable? ". . . and the beam can be adjusted as needed, and what's more, the fact it's tiltable makes it possible to focus the light into the distance. This head-lamp is rightfully called the flashlight of the new millennium."

I'm speechless. The young lady flashes her eyes at me, doubtlessly powered by one lithium CR2 battery, and lowers her voice empathetically: "May I ask what you're going to need it for?"

I'm mute, as if my tongue's been cut out, presumably by the Opinel Outdoor N10 knife in the adjacent display case. Can I really tell her it's for dumpster diving?

"The range," she asks me with a new hint of impatience in her voice, "what sort of range do you need?"

A meter at most. To the bottom of a garbage can.

I stagger to the exit, sweat trickling down my meager cleavage. The Depths pub is next door. It was here not so long ago, or was it ages ago, that I got wasted with some lush quickly and efficiently. "Are you afraid of getting old?"

I order goulash and strong Master dark beer, which finally dims my bulb. I'd like to hear a human voice, I'd like so much for someone to sit down next to me again, but everyone here is scrolling through their phones, diving masks over their eyes and mute butterfly nets over their mouths.

The filaments in the lights continue to quiver.

Bonfire I

And several past, present, and future nights contracted into one, coiled up like a porcupine into a prickly ball, and there was someone skewered on each spine, quill, rapier of the creature in that dream Alice had, relatives, close friends, complete strangers and celebrities alike, and Alice was pulling them off the spines, healing their wounds with her breath and commanding them: "Form a circle around the fire, around this bonfire, and burn whatever you want, throw into the flames whatever it is you need to."

And they obeyed, all those gathered in the fire's glow on the small, hidden beach surrounded by cliffs full of crevices, chasms, geological fissures, and countless caves, on the beach where Alice and Dylan lived in a giant shipping container with a tambourine lying in the corner.

The first to muster the courage was Proust. Due to a fatal printing error, Gennady Musatov's illustrations to Dostoevsky's *The Brothers Karamazov* went astray and ended up in the Czech edition of *In Search of Lost Time*, translated by Prokop Voskovec, and below each illustration was a sentence further illustrating the illustration, for instance "Judge us together! — Grushenka kept shouting, still on her knees." And so the devastated author methodically tore out the illustrations one by one, consigning them to the flames.

A famous model didn't think twice before ripping off her entire face disfigured by Botox, apparently under the impression that her true face would appear underneath, but everyone was surprised to see just a rectangle of smoothed out tinfoil.

And then there was my erstwhile friend and boss who'd devoted all his time to hockey. The others shouted "Go, Jágr, go!" at him mockingly, which wasn't the slightest bit funny, even Proust joined the shrill cheering, as if nobody had noticed the poor sod had two hockey sticks for arms, and so they just looked on dully and indifferently as he poked them into the embers, and they burned up so fast he damn near went up in flames himself.

But my sister Nadia was already puffing her way here, dragging from somewhere all the way to the auto-da-fé huge panels that were from an exhibition she was curating, about Bedřich Smetana, and the flames eagerly lapped at Mařenka's folk skirts and Kecal's ridiculous hairdo from the first staging of *The Bartered Bride*, which took place in 1913 in the open air of Šárka Park, and then my mother flung in our antique Christmas decorations and, God only knows why, her false teeth to boot, so that her face immediately shrank by half.

And finally, finally President Klaus plucked from some unsightly lint the Czech Republic out of Europe, squeezed it in his fist, and tossed the remains, pathetically fizzling out, into the flames.

Alice woke up and stepped outside the container. Dylan's tambourine was lying on the extinguished beach. An enormous ball of fire was slowly emerging from the ocean horizon. Alice's dream touched her with its black head like a match and flared up for a moment before vanishing without a trace.

March 5, 2012

I didn't lock my basement apartment and just slammed the door on my way out. This time, it wasn't a snake slithering toward me down the hallway between the basement stalls, no flat, wary head closing in on me, it was my past. It amounted to the same thing: it drew nearer, hissing and undulating toward me upon its smooth, provocative belly. Walking was as difficult for me as it was for my past — we barely managed to hobble off together to the nearby playground.

Míra and Bobeš sent tumbling down the slide whatever they laid their hands on, and the clanging and screeching seemed endless: forgotten sand molds, empty cola bottles, cans, sticks, stones.

"Auntie, do you want any African marigold seeds like last year?" He shoved a container of Antiperle mints into my hands. I had no idea this round memory was still available.

"Will you help me paint the iron bars blue?" His eyes lit up as if my offer had set off the right switch within him. "Are you still flunking Czech?" Why was I even asking that? I didn't give a damn about Míra's grades. Or did I? I had offered to tutor him some time ago but his mother said no: she obviously saw me as some sort of lonely, shabby, sick weirdo. Bullseye.

I turned my face toward the sun and closed my eyes. The sounds grew stronger. The children yelling and dogs barking, the bangs and voices created a thunderous prelude containing the seeds of all future motifs. A mother started to scream, "Stop throwing that gravel down the slide, damn it!" — and in that moment, my past spread out before me like an enormous sandbox and I squatted down into it and started to grab the colorful plastic sand molds at random, some in the shape of landscapes and others with the profile of a face loved long ago, and my hand came across many mortifying incidents, even my brother's death.

I packed them all down tight, using my scoop with care, evening them out, and turned them over onto the curb. While the contours of some memories were preserved and stayed intact, others collapsed and blended together.

Unasked, the sun pressed its lips to my ear: "Your body does not belong to you. In the words of a poet — ingenious concept, terrible execution. It has never belonged to you. But the iron bars will look good in blue."

Greece bailout hangs in the balance, creditors are reluctant to forgive debts. Are wedding bells in Madonna's future? Her young beau has popped the question. I slept with Kočí, a mysterious witness stated before the Vít Bárta trial. Girl hangs herself because of acne. Fun tips for March: make sure not to miss out on wine tasting and the exhibition of corpses.

Heroin

An obese woman spanned two chairs in Doctor Gnuj's waiting room, which had something quite out of the ordinary for waiting rooms — a piano. Lou Reed was in the middle of rasping out "Heroin" from the radio on top of the piano. I figured I could try to play at least the first two bars of the *Moonlight Sonata*. The obese lady flipped her way through *Today's Woman* magazine like an automaton, a slight pause noticeable only when she came to a recipe.

The walls, the carpet, the chairs, that predominant brown-pink color raping everything here — surely it's supposed to mean something, symbolize something, surely it's supposed to evoke a pleasant atmosphere . . . I might end up changing my mind about the iron bars, and instead of blue choose this womb-like color.

The woman rested on two chairs. The woman rested on three chairs. The woman, suddenly resembling a brown-pink

larva, filled up the entire space, leaving no elbowroom whatso-
ever, and it was obvious she hadn't the slightest interest in
heroin.

"How are you?"

"Not that great, actually."

Silence. Doctor Gnuj said nothing. We both said nothing.
Two portraits hung on the wall above the psychiatrist's head.
Freud and Jung. An eternity passed, and Gnuj swung back in
his ergonomic armchair, tilted his head back in a moment
of epiphany, and clutched at the goatees of his role models:
"How about we try Mirtazapine? Or Valdoxan? Or even . . .
trazodone?"

He closed his eyes at the last word, overcome with delight.

Of course, I couldn't let that go: "Or meth? Or maybe fudge
or sludge or heroin?"

In a heady rush of inspiration, the psychiatrist started to
bang away at his computer. All ten fingers. It lasted a minute,
five, ten. The silence fermented, a recipe in *Today's Woman*. In
it I could hear the chairs cracking and breaking under the
obese woman in the waiting room, all at once, and maybe not
just them, but all seats, couches, kneelers, prie-dieux, pews,
ergonomic armchairs and sofas and adjustable beds and chair
rungs.

All ten of his fingers were typing, tapping away, and I
couldn't, shouldn't take a peek at the text that clearly had
absolutely nothing to do with me.

"I have no money," I said to keep the conversation going. "I
have no money, no job, no family. Apart from Alice, that is,
who's found lifelong love in the flap of a discarded wallet in a
dumpster, and my sister, Nadia, whose sets all burned down."

And suddenly, with no warning, Doctor Gnuj quite unexpectedly fixed on me his brown-pink gaze, matching the waiting room, the gaze of a polyp: "Your inner world is like that basement lair of yours. Kick down the doors, file through the bars! Do you even notice the world around you?"

I do. Don't you worry. I know well enough what the world around me lives for: the season of wine tastings and exhibitions of corpses.

La Nausée

I'm in Tesco, standing in front of the shelves of dairy products, using my reading glasses to examine the ingredients of Bio Olma yogurt: it's produced in strict accordance with the rules and regulations (yes, really, in accordance with rules and regulations!) for organic dairy produce from certified organic farms: milk, powdered milk, milk protein, average nutritional value per 100 grams . . .

A firm tentacle suddenly wraps around me and I hear a thunderous voice behind me: "Běda! Běda!" ("Woe, woe").

I turn around. Isn't that . . . Melda! He's smiling like a clay Buddha, the smile I recognize him by, like that of a child who just got a puppy, beaming like a total idiot, and I realize he wasn't shouting "Běda" but "Běta," my name. He always did have a bit of a speech impediment.

We met five years ago in the neurological ward of the Thomayer Hospital. While he had a tumor the size of a lemon removed from his brain, there was nothing wrong with me — there never was anything wrong with me, just some trivial queasiness, just a laughable case of nausea, *naufragium*, which means shipwreck, just regularly occurring disgust — like so many others, I simply became addicted to the white coat, and through no effort of my own even ended up in a premium room with fridge, shower, and TV.

As the only two smokers, we befriended each other on the terrace with its view of the treetops, beyond which we could make out other allied smokers on other terraces of other wards, also with views of the garden in which some baffling creatures docilely strolled about, ibex, degenerate reindeer, maybe chamois or mouflons or simply even-toed hoofed animals of the Bovidae family, living off bloody hospital refuse and our cigarette butts.

One time, a hulk of an old man showed up on the terrace wearing an ankle-length bathrobe covered in red maple leaves, yes, he was wearing the Canadian flag, and he said, awestruck: "They've become overpopulated in Canada, we're allowed to cull them, but that even here, in Prague . . ." He then pulled binoculars out of the large pocket of his robe and, enthralled, zoomed in on the furless animals whose name remained a secret to us.

But Melda and I were already in a hurry to get back to my premium room, because the four-hundred-and-seventy-fifth episode of the *Critique of Dialectical Reason* series was about to start.

"Běda, nudding is sacred do you, is id," he would say whenever I laughed during inappropriate moments, which was all the time, and immediately fall asleep.

"Buy me dis yogurd please, dad one. And dis ding doo."

Whatever he points out I add to the cart, I'm happy to see him again after so long.

"I god no job, my ID god sdolen, I sleep in duh basemend of

dis one apardmend building, I god screws in my fuhd and spine and duh lemon is gedding bigger again."

He stinks like hell. We slowly roll down the aisle that holds eighty-nine assorted dairy products until we finally arrive after five kilometers at the checkout counters. I have two fifty-crown coins in my pocket, and Melda fishes out a scrounged twenty from the depths of his old pants he's had since his first tramping twenty-three years ago. But the Harpies at the checkout counters, half-women and half-bird, those goddesses of storm winds, let us pass through without a fuss, as though we were two transparent fly wings passing them, the crackling wing-cases of nothingness.

"You'll crash at my place, take a shower. And I'm not gonna sleep with you."

Melda nods obediently. We walk out of the supermarket and freeze: what used to be the parking lot is now an alley of trees, leading from the store and winding into the distance. Left and right, feeble willows with braids lean away from us, resembling figurines in an ethnographic museum. Yet when I look closer — Melda is dealing with problems of his own, hauling the shopping in pain from the screws in his body — I see we aren't surrounded by trees at all, but by broomsticks driven into the ground handle-first, brooms and mops: like skeletons, banshees, and macabre figures, they line our way, and we lift our knees high, way up high like flamingos to step over the odd root jutting into the air.

"Gimme that," I grab the backpack with the food from Melda. "You should get a cane, crutches, or an umbrella at least. You're a cripple, Melda."

"We're cripples," he nods.

We sit down on a tree stump and train our eyes on one of the serpentine roots. It plunges into the ground right under our feet. We no longer even realize it's a root — words disappear, those pronounced correctly and those twisted like that root, and with them the meaning of things, their usage, the faint signs people have sketched onto their surface.

A snake or a claw or a root or a talon, it makes no difference. Melda suddenly bends forward and vomits on it several indigestible chunks of time.

At least a single stem

The sound of drumming was coming from my neighbors in the building next door at regular intervals, and with it dull, hollow blows. Through the crack of an open window I could see the bellowing mouth of a man missing his two front teeth. Míra dangled over his lap, over his father's legs, like a piece of laundry hanging with other clothes on a line stretched across the room diagonally, his eyes vacant as he limply endured his beating.

The shattered slide.

Caught stealing mints at the corner store.

Another F for spelling.

I cravenly averted my eyes to the opposite sidewalk and froze: an ambulance, cops . . . two undertakers were zipping up a bag with a dead man, and the bag — the most striking thing about this whole tableau — wasn't black, as I'd have expected, but white like those stolen mints. I managed to catch a glimpse of the man's face at the last moment. Death. What's it like? Is there at least a single stem growing from here to there and from there to here, one single, spring-shy blade of grass?

It occurred to me that these two incidents were connected, a beating and death, they had to be connected, but I immediately felt ashamed for this wretched idea: nothing is connected to anything. Absolutely no connections at all. Everything in the world happens in parallel, and nothing ever intersects anywhere.

Wine tasting

and the body. How quickly and quietly the zipper closes! There's nothing whiter than this white. And this reality defies understanding over all others: it has always been shabby, the body, mine, still alive, and the lifeless one of that unknown man, from the very beginning. Even then, when they first pulled it on us and drew it up tight to the neck like a noose so we could hardly breathe, even then, when they stood us before the mirror and laid the adulation on thick, how goddamn fantastic we looked and what goddamn hunks and hotshots we were, we just had to go out into the world, even then, this body was already just shabby tatters.

Hambalka

My paternal grandmother lived to be ninety-five. She lived her entire life in the village of Majdalena, and they say the farthest she'd ever been was Třeboň. She raised four children, tended to the farmstead and the apple garden, and fed a multitude of hogs. Each time she held a bucket under Tony's slit throat, because every hog was named Tony, tears would escape from her tightly shut eyes.

Come Sunday, she would attend services held in the local tavern for congregants of the Czechoslovakian Church of Brethren. Her copy of the Bible had been so well-thumbed over the years, read so many times, that it was a shapeless mass, no longer resembling a book but Grandma's own heart, its aorta jutting out of the building and arching over it like a rainbow.

"Dana dear, if only you knew how much I look forward to seeing him," she dreamed out loud on her deathbed, and that image of Jesus, which spread through her as she uttered these words, in which each color was simultaneously the tone of a harmonium and each tone a number of a Bible verse, would forever remain hidden from me, as though I had gone blind myself, holding a bucket filled with blood.

Grandpa didn't have a Bible, he had clocks. They hung everywhere, tick-tocking and discharging stupid cuckoos wherever the eye fell. As a mason, he often traveled around the country for work, and during those times Grandma would immobilize the bobs or wrap an apron around them because Jesus doesn't like the sound of ticking, or drumming, or any dull, hollow blows at regular intervals. Jesus simply hates beatings.

Whenever Grandpa came home from his travels, he'd settle into the hammock strung between two apple trees, bite into an apple until juice gushed, and sigh. He sighed with relish, he sighed even when swallowing, he sighed even while talking, he sighed all the time. My father took after him in this respect, and that's why Grandpa hated him and thought he was an oaf.

One day he gathered his children, a daughter and three sons, to go over who would inherit what once he died. This ritual, well-oiled and punctually maintained, had recurred once a year from the time they were kids. My father though, oblivious to the testament, gazed out the open window at an apple tree and observed its branches for so long, so persistently and obdurately, he turned into wood, he turned into a tree himself and bore that sweet weight of apples.

"And you," Grandpa barked out suddenly, "what is it you want?"

"*Hambalka,*" the branch aimlessly blurted out.

When my father told me this story some time ago, I had to recheck the *Dictionary of Standard Czech:* 1. a horizontal beam connecting roof rafters, also used for drying hay; 2. a hayloft; 3. a wooden pole hung horizontally above the stove for drying laundry.

Grandpa's fist flew out like a birdie from a cuckoo clock and hit my father right between his closed eyes. He had quite rightly deduced that my father was winding him up. Grandma's loving apron covered the house in an instant, it covered the entire town of Majdalena, concealing from view that terrible and boundless municipal district all the way to Třeboň.

"Hamburg" comes right after *hambalka* in the *Dictionary of Standard Czech*.

March 10, 2012

True spring will come with March, meteorologists are promising up to 17°C.

Tens of thousands protest against Putin in Moscow.

The pregnant daughter of millionaire Michael Kocáb, writer Natálie Kocábová, doesn't even have enough money to buy a stroller.

Kampa Island crouched and barked.

Alžběta ended up sleeping with Melda once he'd showered, and then right after they went back to Tesco for blue metal paint.

The Kikimora

Of course, I had no intention of coming clean to Linda Řádná or the Harpies. Dejectedly, I just opened my hand to reveal the two fifty-crown coins. They clinked against each other like funeral bells, for I had left the question "what do you consider the meaning of your life to be?" unanswered in the questionnaire for the usherette job. I was likewise unsuitable for the position of housekeeper, as would become evident later when visiting some high-end villa in Vokovice, because apparently I looked — so said the owner — like a Shishimora.

Wikipedia soon informed me that this is a female boogieman from Slavic mythology — Kikimora in Czech — a hideous old hag dressed in rags who kidnaps kids.

I couldn't confess to them that I wasn't totally down and out, a stain upon a stain, a louse's louse that'd taken the bait. And so I whispered to the crack extending along the wall, thinner than my mother's lips: I sold everything I could. I sold the piano that in my fifty-four years I learned to play only three pieces on: "Für Elise," the opening adagio of Beethoven's *Moonlight Sonata No. 14*, and that ragtime song from *The Sting*.

I sold the china tea set to a peculiar figure in a shop with an ANTIQUE sign, and if there were anyone who actually looked like a Kikimora, it would have to be her. I stepped inside the shop, the bell above the door jingled, and my mom, who was with me, mischievously whispered in my ear, "Sell me, I'm the greatest antique of 'em all!"

I also sold: two of Grandpa's clocks, nobody will ever manage to coax a cuckoo out of those moldered birds again, a suitcase full of vinyl records that held such black, cracked treasures such as a 1963 recording of *The Greek Passion* by Bohuslav Martinů, and records from the thirties even, hard and brittle like choco-late, 75 RPM, of Stalin's speeches. Excited, the collectors' fingers trembled, and these trembling fingers wove themselves into a tender and safe basket, a wrapping and nest for the tones of music and the voice of a murderer alike.

And finally even a Vladimír Boudník print my parents gave me on my eighteenth birthday. What good was it to me, when the view from the only window in my basement apartment was of a wall with five layers of plaster, flaking away in varying rhythms and time, a wall with the outlines of destroyed cities?

This let me buy Melda a new pair of pants. He swaggered around in them and stomped through that miniature space of mine, my unfurnished apartment where there was nothing for dust to settle on, through that hollow body of a bell where we'd constantly bump and walk into each other, at times trudging aimlessly from wall to wall, through that dump Melda decided to share with me, through that barred cell to which I, thanks to divine favor, had a key, and despite it being my *home*, yes, I emphasize that word deliberately, it didn't change a damn thing about our homelessness.

From time to time Melda would pull some book from the shelf, itself full of holes like my nightie, open it at random and start to recite out loud like a first grader, carefully and monot-onously, "I'd jus like do find a brudder or sisder who see id like I do and feel id wid me . . ."

Once though, I didn't understand why, his speech impedi-ment suddenly disappeared: "Nobody ever gets used to a con-stant feeling of injustice, not the nation, not a city, not even the private individual. Never gets used to it, never makes peace with it, but merely brings the anger down to a simmer, becomes small and sour, silent and sad, starts to slouch and loses hope. Small and sour, slouching and sad, silent and hopeless was the city of Prague . . ."

"This can't continue," I interrupted him. "You're gonna buy a tram ticket, take the 17 to Výstaviště, what used to be called Julius Fučík Park of Culture and Leisure, and stand with the guys who hang around the railing, smoking and waiting for someone to come along and hire them for the day. It's usually Ukrainians or Russians who show up. I'll teach you one sentence in Russian, repeat that and nothing else. I'll be heading out to the employment office in a little while. Everything's changed. You understand? Everything. The Minister of Social Affairs has merged the Department of Social Welfare with the labor offices, and now there is unbelievable chaos everywhere and the names of the civil servants are no longer listed on the doors, who knows what happened to Linda Řádná, now they're labeled by months. You know that fairy tale about the Twelve Months? I'm March. As for that sentence in Russian . . . Make sure to remember it: My name is Melda and I am good at all sorts of fabrication."

He started to repeat it obediently, but paused in surprise: "Fabrication?" he repeated skeptically.

"Yeah, fabrication!"

I heard clear as day all the screws in his body loudly creak.

Worms and string theory

Yes. I was left here with almost nothing in the hollow of this bell bereft of tongue, nothing for dust to settle on, just a mattress, a bare-bones kitchen unit, rising and falling like a graph, and instead of a desk a baking sheet propped up on two bricks, a baking sheet for strudel and Christmas cookies that now supported a computer too old to sell.

From time to time it would simply shut down, die, go dark, and I'd be left staring blankly at the reflection of my own face instead of an email from Alice.

"Dear Mom, it's an incredible 20°C here, quite a shock after spending Christmas with you guys. When I went out to get water, there was a snake on the narrow path basking in the sun, so I just stepped over it and didn't even look back, maybe this also was a dream. It's weird, I didn't dream of anything at all in Prague, but here . . . like today: our eleven-story apartment block in Modřany. I think of it often. I wonder who's living there now. What our old apartment looks like? Which parts of the Formica paneling in the bathroom are rotting away, where we used to — remember? — sit in the bathtub and passionately argue about the existence of God when I was twelve, thirteen, fourteen!

"And each floor in this dream was one European city. Brussels on the third, Paris on the seventh, Madrid on the tenth, and Prague on the last, eleventh, floor. When I took the elevator to the basement, I found myself in Třeboň, and I don't know why it seemed the most distant city of them all. The names of the cities were written above the elevator buttons, and I rode from one metropolis to another however I felt like it, but I never stepped off at Brussels because it bored me, and I also didn't go down to Třeboň, because I was scared . . ."

Suddenly, darkness. And my face in the mirror of the dead monitor.

"Yesterday Bob and I pried open this one dumpster. Right at the top was this huge, wilted bouquet and a box of chocolates underneath it wrapped in fancy paper, with lots of frills and ribbons. The dumpster was standing in front of this house, and only one ground-floor window was lit up, no shadows behind the curtains, no signs of life.

"'I bet it was her birthday,' I wondered aloud, and Bob continued, 'Yeah. It was her birthday and he was bringing her flowers and a box of chocolates.'

"'She wasn't expecting him . . .'

"'She thought he was in Grenada attending a training for insurance agents.'

"'He was planning to surprise her . . .'

"'She'd given him the key only two weeks before, that was a mistake . . .'

"'He came in, and in the same bed they'd recently made love in she was with a stranger. Both naked . . .'

"'He noticed the odd, revolting gleam of their bodies, how they no longer resembled humans but worms after the rain, completely covered in lube . . .'

"'. . . so gross. He set down the chocolates and bouquet — a cheery mix of multicolored tulips — on the shoe cabinet, and went to the kitchen to grab a knife, first-rate Solingen steel used for filleting fish . . .'"

Darkness once more. But only for a few seconds — only for a few seconds, the story continued through my wide eyes and several tenuous contours of my face, "'. . . and he slit both the worms' throats.'

"We left the bouquet and Bob grabbed the chocolates, he has a mean sweet tooth.

"'I could use a new wallet, mine's falling apart,' I said and dug into the dumpster again. I wasn't surprised at all when I managed to pull one out in no time. It was a brand new red leather wallet with a thousand flaps for a thousand gold credit cards.

"'And there might be fifty euros in it.' I rifled through its compartments and hardly managed to stammer out, 'Bob, just thirty . . .'

"The ground-floor window went dark.

"On the way back, Bob tore through the decorative paper and broke into his spoils, and while he was picking the chocolates out of their nests, he started to explain string theory to me. For one thing, I'd always had bad grades in physics, as you know, and for another, my English really isn't good enough to grasp the topic, and to top it off he was talking with his mouth full, so I can only say this from his explanation: there are nine dimensions, six of which are rolled up, so to speak. I think he used the word *swaddle*, not *roll up*. Maybe tonight I will finally muster enough courage to go to Třeboň."

I must've pressed some key by accident, because a picture of a twisted necklace made of plastic beads appeared on the screen, and below it the caption: "One of the amino acids that is the precursor to DNA."

The first molecular structures were born in interstellar space before appearing on Earth by way of falling meteorites. CNRS research thus shows that life on Earth originated in outer space.

Melda hadn't come back yet. Day was breaking. Birds were already starting to shriek, and stems, growing from God knows where to God knows where, protruded from the seashell of dawn like caricatures of Venus.

March 18, 2012

Eleven-year-old prostitutes in Bangladesh swallow Oradexon tablets used to fatten up livestock.

Green faceless men have started to enforce payments from debtors.

In basement stall number twelve, an old sled was biding its time for a new mountain.

The augur

It'd been a few days since Melda vanished off the face of this earth. I imagined where he could be wandering, simmering in his anger, unappeased, in which Prague district had he become small and sour, silent and sad, slouched and hopeless.

I wished the lemon in his head were not a lemon but just a blueberry, or not even a blueberry but a speck of dust that, like in my apartment, had nowhere to settle on in the emptiness of his head. And hoping for this fruity metamorphosis, I managed to visit the neurology and rheumatology departments in the Women's Home and to even squeeze in a mammography.

While preparing the syringes for a localized injection, the neurologist barked, "And the McKenzie method — tried it yet?"

I lay down on my stomach obediently and stretched my torso up as far as my lower back would allow. But the doctor was still unsatisfied: "Higher, farther! Higher, farther!" she shouted at me, as if she were instructing me from below on how to scale a climbing wall.

Uneven rails began to run through my back instead of my spine, an aged local train rattling along painfully, where my grandma sat in her Sunday pinafore, a headscarf tied under her chin. For the first and last time, having no idea she was right then passing through her granddaughter's body, she was traveling from Majdalena to the fair in Třeboň. Somewhere in the fields beyond the village my back popped and that was the end of that.

Two women sat in the waiting room, one old and thin, the other young and fat. The fat one had tears rolling down her cheeks. I thought she was quite understandably daunted by the McKenzie method, but the cause of her terror was much worse. It was not even half an hour ago that a woman had jumped from a fifth-floor window of the Women's Home. The body had landed right next to her. She saw the brains gush out of the cracked skull onto the asphalt.

"I saw the brain, I saw the brain," she repeated over and over, as if the unexpected death she'd witnessed closed her into an egg with no way to escape. "I'll always see that brain . . ."

I staggered into the pharmacy for some Diclofenac, 50 mg per one enteric-coated tablet. I swallowed a handful of the brown lozenges on the spot. The train rattling along my spine was now a sinuous river winding through Prague like my neighbor's escaped snake, that painful, scoliotic Vltava undulating under bridges and along muddy waterfronts, suddenly full of inorganic trash, blueberries and mints, strawberries and rotting rags, moldering tires and festering bouquets and spilled brains.

In the park above Anděl, a paradise for losers and junkies, bearing the ironic name Sacré-Coeur, Melda sat with several of his buddies, drunk as a skunk. They sat around on the grass still hard, humid, and cold from the winter, and their stench wafted all the way to me from their circle of wine boxes and PET bottles as if it were some black magic ritual.

"For cryin' out loud, where've you been? I made you goulash," I let fly at him like a proper housewife.

"I met a bird collector."

What's he babbling about?

"I went where you sent me. In about two hours' time a Benz pulled up to me, tinted windows, the guy behind the wheel dressed all in black . . ."

Melda's buddies started to squabble among themselves over something, not interested in the story they'd evidently already heard ten times over.

"We drove who knows where, the windows were darkened . . ." It occurred to me that Melda didn't have a fruit in his brain, but his brain in a fruit. "The guy was on the phone the entire time, talking to someone in Finnish."

"Finnish? How'd you know it was Finnish?"

"Excuse me," he objected, "I'm still capable of recognizing Finnish, thank you very much!"

Since a certain moment in time Melda had stopped mixing up his speech sounds. Something was happening. Something was in the air, and the bums started to clap their hands and dance to music that suddenly came toward us from the nearby budding young natural scientists refuge where two kangaroos were being reared.

"The gate opened in front of us automatically and we noiselessly drove up the graveled driveway . . ." It was suspiciously starting to resemble an opening scene from some Chandler detective story.

". . . to an immense, white, angular chateau."

"Must've been some functionalist villa . . ." I tried to knock Melda's yarn into reality. But it was no use. What's more, the bums had now changed into kangaroos and were jumping in and out of each other's pouches.

"An enormous aviary stood in the garden. He led me to it, opened the hatch in the mesh, and shoved me inside. 'Tomorrow morning you'll tell me what's in store for me,' he said. 'You'll be able to tell by the flight of birds. And their song. You're a bird oracle. Understand? An augur.'"

"More like a birdbrain and nutcase, if anything," one of them sniggered as he gallantly passed me the bottle.

I drank the wine like water, I drank it in one go until finally everything became covered in a transparent plastic wrap, every object, every blade of grass, every rooftop of the city spread out below us, someone had shrink-wrapped them firm and airtight, like luggage at the airport.

"I wanted to tell him that it's gotta be some mistake, that he musta confused me with somebody else, that I don't know jack about birds and besides — what am I supposed to tell from their flight when they can hardly fly in that cage! 'If you fulfill the task, you shall leave with the Mercedes we came in. Should you fail, however . . .' This is really how he talked, no kidding. I wouldn't be able to come up with this even if I wanted to! Just then the Czech anthem started to play. His phone was ringing. He didn't finish telling me what would happen to me if I . . . and he launched into Finnish again. He locked me in with those critters and leisurely walked away in the direction of the white chateau. Two vultures in buckskin leggings were sizing me up with a sinister look in their eye and pointing their beaks at me like bayonets."

I had to lie down for a while in the circle of wine boxes, even though a chilly wind was blowing and the ground was cold. I wanted to touch my face, arms, legs, to make sure that it was still me. That what I lay on was still the ground, that my being hadn't floated off — but it wasn't possible to touch myself: my body, too, was tightly wrapped in plastic.

"I walked along the mesh looking for a hole of any kind. I was hungry. I dug into the bucket of grain, it was pretty easy to chew and tasted like rolled oats. I tore off a piece of raw meat from a branch and drank from the water feeder. To tell a stranger's future from bird flight? They sat on the branches so still they looked like mounted animals. From their song? They stuffily remained silent, not a single chirp, and gawked at me with hatred in their eyes like when a new prisoner is brought to his cell. 'You'll get nothing out of us,' one of the vultures with buckskin leggings suddenly said in the voice of my dad, 'no future. Not his,' twisting his beak with contempt in the direction of the chateau, 'not that of a single chromosome. Simply because no future exists. There's just the here and now, a continuous, fluid tone the color of brick.'"

"Didn't he mean to say prick, this pecker of yours?"

"Or dick?"

His buddies started to roar with laughter and scattered across the expanse of Sacré-Coeur, not caring about the marvelous, unusual view it offered of Prague, of a city full of injustice that nobody ever got used to, not the nation, not the private individual. In short, they'd become sour and plunged their arms elbow-deep into garbage cans, and when they pulled them out again, they were the color of melted chocolate.

"I woke up on a bench in Stromovka Park. I'd shoved a bread roll into my pocket and now crumbs were falling out of it. There musta been a hundred pigeons flapping their wings around me, their heads nodding up and down like mechanical birds, pecking at the bread roll like their lives depended on it."

The shriek of a bird suddenly came out of nowhere. First one, then another. In no time cawing and squawking was all around us, one bird after another joined in with both cacophony and harmony coming out of their beaks, until it was impossible to hear one's own words on the hill above Anděl, until their clamor settled upon the city and drowned it out completely.

The wretches who'd been romping around froze, began to pick up their plastic bags, and staggered off in the direction of Holečkova Street.

Only Melda and I remained, bewitched by that avian racket. Melda looked triumphant, straight-up smug, as though the singing of the birds that had broken out in the aviary abutting the kangaroo cage at the young natural scientists refuge was some sort of proof that he'd done as I'd told him, that he'd really been waiting that morning three days ago in front of Výstaviště for someone to hire him for a temp job, and that he'd been so close, so very close, to having in the pocket of those new pants I'd bought him the keys to that Mercedes instead of a crumbled bread roll.

The Rorschach test

Countless times I have tried to guess the number of plaster layers on the wall across from my window. In places it has crumbled away down to the brick, in other spots it seems to have made one last attempt to clothe this skeleton — in a noxious yellow-green color. Mostly though, the colors have blended together, pink with baby blue, white with gray meanders. I'd straddle a chair, lean my elbows against the windowsill, and for hours and days, weeks and seconds, immerse myself in those colors, from the top layers to the brick bone, to the very foundation, the mysterious core of that house crumbling away, its windows covered over by particleboard, rotting away day by day like an apple in autumn, which also mysteriously changes color, as though each new hue were born, created, and grew out of the previous one.

I couldn't fathom how this singular ruin appeared in the middle of the tidy, constantly spruced-up Na Homolce apartment complex. Did the same person try to replaster it over and over again in a single lifetime, each time in the state of mind, the mood, the season of a different color? Or did the building change owners with its colors?

No, I really can't complain about where I live. I have a complete range of public facilities nearby: two hospitals, numerous pharmacies, a cemetery, even a crematorium.

In the blots, in the crooked islands, I can spot more changes and shapes than if I were observing clouds. And not just the outline of an animal long extinct, the orifice of a screaming mouth, or the ultrasound image of my yet unborn Alice, I see much, much more: an erupting volcano burying villages in scalding lava and fine ash, South American slums with shacks growing dank, women buried neck-deep into the ground, a man running through the street with his dead son in his arms — all of it swirling on the wall of the building opposite my window, on the only true, real screen I have the courage to turn on from time to time.

Sometimes, though, a merciful fog settles on the building. The tableaux, too tangible to bear, turn into colorful abstractions, as if I've screwed my eyes shut and perceive only a play of colors and shapes behind them. And suddenly I recall how my mom took me to see a psychologist once, I was twelve or thirteen and maybe even weirder back then than I am now, I don't really remember, even memory is just a play of colors and shapes behind eyelids shut in a desire for non-existence. He showed me some pictures, ink blots symmetrical along a vertical axis running through the center of the card. Did it remind me of anything? Was I supposed to let my imagination run wild? What swaddled dimensions, what unknowable universes existed back then, just like today, between my mental images and the words I was forced to use to express them?

Indeed: the infamous Rorschach test.

"A blot," I told the psychologist when he showed me the first card, but I imagined horse shit on a forest path, which was very strange, given the path was so narrow, no horse could possibly squeeze its way down it.

"Okay, but what does the blot remind you of?"

"A blot."

"And this picture?"

"A blot. A blot. A blot."

It reminded me of the noble profile of Old Shatterhand's face, it reminded me of a human brain and a singed map of Prague, it reminded me of . . . But why in the world should I tell him that? Just like today, I stubbornly insisted on words quite different to those bursting inside me like bubbles on the water's surface.

Melda's lying on a foam mattress and drinking no euro-rotgut but the good Chilean wine he'd given me for my birthday. He drinks it all in one go, being an alcoholic. And me? A blot. Behind the closed eyelids of God knows who. Blots.

Straddling the chair, my eyes fixated on them like on the pages of Chandler's *The Lady in the Lake*. "Noiselessly and slowly, he drove up the graveled driveway . . ."

"The body, creaking in collapse, ingenious concept, terrible execution," Melda recites from a different book altogether.

"You better not pawn my PC, you bastard with jack shit in his pocket, keys to a Benz my ass."

Yes, it's true. I acquired Melda like an animal that doesn't understand my words, and so I can tell him anything, I can curse at him or recite poetry to him, yes, I acquired him like an enormous pot into which I can toss my undigested, blotted life, all that I can no longer stomach.

"Just imagine, you wretch, when I was twelve, thirteen, my mom took me to see a psychologist. He measured my IQ, it was only slightly higher than a dolphin's. And then he started to show me pictures . . . You better not drink away my computer, ya hear me! Then you'd never find out about the Rorschach test. And that Herman Rorschach first presented it to the medical public in 1921, and that C.G. Jung helped him create it. The Rorschach test consists of ten cards with colored blots. All the inkblots are symmetrical along the vertical axis running through the center of the card. Even Leonardo da Vinci himself was interested in random blots and cracks in the walls, imagine that! But today both the validity and reliability of the test have been called into question. Nor does the Rorschach test assess sexual orientation. Nevertheless, it still remains one of the most widely used psychological methods. For instance, in forensic medicine it is the second most utilized method. Approximately six million people worldwide are subjected to this test every year."

The minute I stop talking, workers arrive and start to construct scaffolding on the building opposite, and an unfamiliar polyp floats through the room, through that blankness where there's nothing for dust to settle on.

Floors

Ever since they started putting up scaffolding around that mysterious ruin, Melda became more organic. He'd stand stock-still in front of the window, listening attentively, concentrating on the pealing pipes as if it were the *Moonlight Sonata*, and wouldn't take his eyes off the workers' hands, not for a single moment. He simply stopped blinking, so he turned into a fish, a flounder, an octopus, a sturgeon. Sturgeons don't have eyelids and neither did he, for his eyes resembled pits made by horses' hooves, potholes flooded with water. He watched rigidly as the levels of scaffolding rose up, one floor after another. And when the fifth one had been put up, he said: "Flour."

"Floor," I corrected him.

"This used to be my job. I used to work as a scaffolder. And once . . . It was on the fifth floor, and I could see through a window with no curtains straight into a living room. There was this group of folks having a good time, know what I mean, everybody was naked, bodies all tangled together, I never seen anything like it, maybe in a porno film, I pressed my cheek against the windowpane and just couldn't look away, it was . . . it was strange, not arousing at all, tortuously contorted bodies like photos from an extermination camp, as if they were all long dead even though they were squirming, thrusting, shouting, spreading their legs and baring their butts, and as I stepped back from the window in horror, I fell from the scaffolding and landed on my back. I spent half a year lying in the hospital, here at Motol, where they took out all my bones and replaced them with screws."

"Yeah, I know. You're no longer human, Melda, you're a kind of . . . how to put it . . . a mechanical being . . ." I knew hundreds of poems by heart, it couldn't be helped, that was the way it had to be, it was similar to those screws of Melda's, it would kill me if someone were to remove them from my body, "'. . . oh, body, you beautiful dynamo, imbuing your environs with life . . . ,' you're basically a blender of sorts, a remote-controlled toy car, a coffeemaker or vacuum cleaner."

And, true, even a sturgeon at times, but I didn't want to say it out loud lest the dynamo's head swell.

The workers left as soon as they'd finished erecting the scaffolding, and the ruin was deserted once more. But the vacuum cleaner found a new source of entertainment — he began to piece together coffee tables and stools out of empty wine boxes, even making a cabinet with drawers for clothing and pasting cartons over the floor, which now looked as if covered in cheery parquet, he even covered the walls and ceiling and then finished up by crafting gorgeous, stylish lampshades for the bare light bulbs.

We've been living inside a wine box ever since, in a thoroughly drained, baffling, stiff, reinforced space.

And then one day the glasses in the vitrine of this cardboard cabinet suddenly seemed to have wilted and loudly cracked, and an unknown voice said: "Now it's your turn. Become translucent, delicate as a breeze, and let others drink from you."

I replied to another twenty-five job offers today, and as I was about to answer the twenty-sixth the screen went dark and I spotted the reflection of my face, which was, just like Melda's creation, thoroughly drained, baffling, angular, and utterly unemployable. In this endless battle of blots, in this deathly boring ten-card game, all I can do is describe it with words quite different to those inside me, words that are delicate, breezy, and translucent, just like the unknown voice requested.

March 20, 2012

The Top Five Regrets of the Dying, a book written by Australian hospice nurse Bronnie Ware, has become an international bestseller.

First storks arrive a week earlier than expected.

The Vltava gushes out of a cracked egg.

Ash Wednesday, on a Friday in March

"Mom, a dream today. About you. Your legs were two tree trunks, you grew right into the ground in Stromovka Park. You cowered between an elm and a willow tree, I knew it was an elm even though I have no idea what one looks like. People walking their dogs passed you, people on roller skates and on bikes and on crutches passed you, and none of them noticed that you weren't a tree, they simply thought you were just another tree among trees, and I had to do it, when I wanted to set you free, I had to take an ax and cut off, chop off, both your legs just above the ground until only two bloody stumps were left. But all those years! All those bloodied growth rings! And seconds beyond count.

"A jet of spurting crimson sap flung you toward some children who happened to be walking by with their two teachers, a kindergarten on an outing, heading toward the monkeys bars, and your hobbling torso joined them, the kids began to shriek in horror when they saw you, and you started to whip them one after the other, you flailed away with your branches, and then suddenly the whole of Stromovka Park along with everything in it coiled into a snake, into a gigantic cobra that reared its telescope-like head and raised itself high up into the air, so high up that its head then formed a living, quivering rooftop over the Petřín Observation Tower, over the entire city —"

The screen went dark. And in that sudden, unexpected darkness, the torso of the dream and the stumps of reality, these eternal siblings grappling with each other unexpectedly embraced.

I went out into the night, and suddenly, a small light in the distance kept getting closer and larger, the murmuring wind and sea in its wake, yes, the actual sea, Alice, here at the Na Homolce apartment complex right behind the cemetery, it murmured softly wherever I went, and suddenly everything that had ever existed was contained in that round light: words and days, the arm in a cast, and familiar faces, all those longing gazes of a wretched maggot directed skyward, extending its maggot head as far back as possible, as far as the gargoyles of St. Vitus Cathedral, as far as the gargoyles of Notre Dame that I admired back in the day, monsters much more sublime.

O vain reason that furtively tries
to make us understand the stream that rushes us ever onward,
and like the yearning of a cathedral, propels us into towers,
            we maggots of the earth.

The light zipped by and disappeared — a night biker sporting a headlamp rode past.

And back home again that voice, wavering between falsetto

and bass, alternating, turning into a woman's and child's voice and before long into the trembling voice of an old man, asking: "Are you afraid of getting old?"

What could I say to that? I'm eroding, as slowly and inescapably as a cliff.

"Your hair's turned gray," Melda added mercilessly, "why don't you dye it? And what about getting a chic haircut? You look awful. You look like Cinderella. Stomping on hazelnuts in your fury, but each contains only a maggot and a cobweb and no wishes. All the words you utter, truly all of them are nothing more than your separating peas from ash."

This rude stranger for whom I'd bought whatever he pointed to at Tesco just a few days before was now parading around in his grandiose cardboard box butt naked, and the scars that furrowed his body looked like riverbeds through which time streamed instead of water.

Elms

are deciduous trees comprising the flowering plant genus *Ulmus* in the plant family Ulmaceae. Some individual elms reach great size and age (up to 400 years). The genus first appeared in the Miocene about 40 million years ago. The elm trunk is typically covered in dark, deeply-serrated bark. Its flowers are wind-pollinated, the elm thus belongs among anemophilous plants.

Whatever shines too bright

I wanted to go out, but lying in front of the door was what should never be crossed, lest the punishment thread you a necklace of cells fit for death: flint, bronze, and steel.

The wind pushed along a scrap of unread newspaper, some men in neckties running the world flew over the ground, the eurozone hit a wall, and I managed to glimpse the headline THE INNER WORKINGS OF POLITICAL PARTIES GENERALLY DOES NOT PAINT A VERY PRETTY PICTURE, and Bobeš and Míra trampled all over a Libyan city in ruins — "Did you plant the marigold seeds yet? You gotta cover 'em with lots of soil! And when are we gonna paint the bars?" — and Jágr's bicep flew under a parked Škoda, this was no longer even a wind but a gale, it was a hurricane that raised taxes until they blew up and away and landed on the scaffolding of the opposite building, and such fatigue spilled out of all those newspaper pages, such drowsiness, such death, it was as though each word were a syringe of poison, all the way at the top of the tower of an enchanted castle.

Whatever shines too bright obliterates its own shadow. That's why tonight Melda and I were going to go exploring.

Time

drove me on, spurred me on with kurbash and scourge, whistling and whooping cheerfully until after fifty-four years it drove me with its spurs into a rather ordinary, spacious pen sown with the desiccated grasses of the present. But what kind of pen was it, here amid complete desolation with no sign of a fence anywhere that would enclose this monstrously symmetrical space, festering like the bottom of an old well?

I really did try to follow Doctor Gnuj's advice: "Kick down the doors! File through the bars! Open your eyes, take notice of the reality surrounding you!"

Not only did I notice it, I even started a journal, in secret of course, so Melda wouldn't know, under the working title *Synapse*:

Chickens spend their entire lives within the confines the size of a shoebox.

Pope set to receive Easter gift of consecrated beer from Plzeň.

But now, in this moment, it's not my fault my eyes have turned into two magnifying glasses: everything my new gaze falls upon is magnified many times over, magnified to such a degree that I'm not able to make out what it is I'm actually seeing: the leg of an insect, a monstrously enlarged skin pore, a single curve of the edge of a stamp, or the fragment of a letter that's part of Alice's long email about her dream?

I'm certain of only a single thing: If I'm a wave, I cannot drown like my brother.

Angels

After that wildly successful Christmas dinner we had in that convivial family circle of ours, Alice and I went to Pernink in the Ore Mountains for some cross-country skiing, like we do every year.

I lift the pot lid and stare at the bottom of those days. Where have they gone, where are they now, at this moment, those angels of ours? The spring sun bears down on the freshly painted iron bars of my window, as if it — a county-fair strongman — wants to bend them into a horseshoe. What shape the puddled remains of our angels, which land has absorbed them, which soil has thirstily slurped them up, our snow angels?

You go first, I'll follow in your tracks. It's always been that way. I watch you sleeping in your crib, a rattle in your tiny fist, and even then, you're already walking ahead of me, making way for me.

Whenever I feel like it, I can enter whichever scene I choose, and now it's that endless plain covered in snow that's being stirred up, swirled by wind, a gale, a blizzard of such prowess as if from another time and place, a holey dress train of a blizzard blanketing our tracks in an instant. Chilled to the bone, I trudge in your wake on my skis, angrily skewering the pale, empty sky with the tips of my poles, and I draw myself up straight into the air like a vertical axis and suddenly see lines and strokes in the sky and on the ground, and they aren't the trajectories of planes or ski tracks at all, but actually — I am sure — the crisscrossed strokes of nouns and modifiers.

I want to talk to you, when will I see you again, but the wind is screeching like a choir of old crones.

"Screw this, Mom, we'll never make any headway like this," you shout over the whistling wind and begin to unhook your skis.

In the snowy void.

In the infinite white.

"Come on, let's make snow angels instead!"

What angels?

. . . *yearning for the white, you head into the black darkness where in your bliss maggots keep you company.*

You lie on your back and flap your arms up and down. I remember at last. When we get up again, the imprints of our winged bodies are left in the snow. But not for long: the snow-white gown sweeps them away in an instant, we don't give up though and advance through the snowy plain on our backs, marking it with the shapes of our bodies, again and again, till crooked rows of angels stretch all the way to the horizon, till . . . but where did they go, where are they now, at this moment? What shape was the puddle that absorbed them, which thirsty spring soil slurped them up?

The next day we're building a snowman. I find out something about Bob Dylan.

"He spent ten years working as a DJ in London. He was real good at it, and sometimes an MC (that's a master of ceremony), the girl he was dating, would perform with him. They were constantly shitfaced, you know, high as a kite, totally wrecked at times . . . Know what I mean? Completely out of it, they were snorting coke and dropping molly balls and paper and bombs and X was their daily bread. You can imagine how heavy this shit got, so Bob dumped his MC and his sound mixer and records and took just a couple things and left for Spain in his old van. Eventually . . ."

I already know what happened next. A shipping container in Nerja, Andalusia, Costa del Sol. And Bob in the asana position on a beach.

I'm entranced. By all those new words shooting out of Alice like New Year's fireworks while completely traditional snowmen with carrot noses grow underneath our gloves. My daughter is speaking in a foreign language, unfamiliar to me, she's emitting sounds like when she was still learning to speak, and suddenly I notice that Alice's white golem is towering over mine, that it's again ahead of mine by the width of a body, by a slice of reality, by the whole snowball of cold life itself.

The next day we see the snowmen through the window. Everything's thawing. Water is dripping from icicles and signs reading USE THE OTHER SIDEWALK hang from each house. Our handiwork has coalesced into one snowdrift, into one enormous heap like a dead, washed up, white octopus, into one single fragile being — just like us two, mother and daughter.

Alice, if only you knew how much I miss you. I wish I could be the cove you submerge into as you laugh and yell something at Bob standing on the shore, or that I could manage, at least for a short while, to bear the mire of life like a rose.

My being floated off elsewhere

You're three months old, sleeping in your crib, clutching a rattle in your tiny fist. Andrei is just leaving for his night shift in a boiler room. It's January 18, 1988, ten minutes to ten. The door closes. The apartment falls silent, a tenor wafting through the wall from the neighbors the only sound, the tenor who has kept all of us company our entire lives: "I have to make it on my own . . ."

"My God," I pray over you, "I feel nothing at all. Who are you, you unfathomable creature? Where did you come from? You are a guest. I've given birth to a guest."

With angry amazement in all the concealed recesses of my body, amazement and anger that I'm not like other mothers, I walk to the window in the kitchen of our apartment on the eleventh floor. On the small playground with a sandbox, a streetlight illuminates a bench next to which a male body lies motionless. It has a black jacket like Andrei's. I freeze. A lump in my throat. And my first thought, word, echo: "Punishment!"

Is it him? How can I be sure, looking down at him from such a height?

The ambulance arrives before long. A doctor, orange vests, hurried movement, first aid. I go to your room again, I'm little more than a pounding heart, a puffy lump of dread. I pull out a book at random, one that'll become your favorite in a couple of years, and read out loud: "The hard, green ice turned back into soft pea soup. Owl sat down in his chair and quietly finished his supper. He didn't mind that it was cold one bit."

I return to the window. The man is still lying there inert, but he's alone. Dead. There are seven apartments on each floor of this eleven-story tower block. Eleven times seven. About three inhabitants to an apartment, seventy-seven times three. You wake up bawling and send your rattle flying. What am I supposed to do? I quickly swaddle the small, fragile, crying guest in layers until I wind up with an unreal onion. Elevator going down. To make sure that the dead man isn't Andrei, your father.

It's dark outside. Just that lone streetlight illuminates the bench like the floodlight of a watchtower. Not a living soul in sight. The man is no longer here, just a pack of night hyenas in bathrobes and slippers shuffling around close by, numb with cold.

"Where is he?" I ask.

"The undertakers just took him away."

I clutch the wailing guest tight beneath my coat like a burden, a precious lifelong burden. I pace the apartment for miles that night, my steps unsteady after a handful of sleeping pills that don't work on death. They never did work on death, not even in later years. In the morning, the key rattles in the lock and Andrei is standing in the doorway. Back from his night shift.

Whenever I feel like it, I can enter whichever scene I choose, and today it's that long gone, awful night that wraps and tightens around my neck like a bathrobe belt.

"Melda, hand me a book, doesn't matter which one."

Melda fumbles around in our rickety, wine-box bookcase. I open it at random, just like back then:

For ages I buried myself in books
like a reptile stupefied by heat,
didn't read anyway, just took in the muddle,
my being floated off elsewhere.

Saturday, March 31, 2012, Quido's name day

It's Earth Hour today. The biggest global happening in support of the environment. Will you take part?

An amazing two hours of bowling and fun fun fun, includes two free beers and pizza 61% off!

Alice, please try to explain to Dylan that it's Quido's name day today, and — what a name day is. The English don't have name days. And don't forget to tell him that today the MPs . . . and that the sieve of the sifting pan let light through as soon as dawn broke . . . and that — Owl didn't mind that it was quite cold one bit.

The magnet

My own screaming woke me in the night. Melda claimed I was shouting in a strange male voice: "What are you doing up there? Get down from that sacred tree right this minute and stop being so elusive!"

It's true. From the height of the eleventh floor, although it could also have been, I admit, an eleven-storied sacred tree, I was looking down at my neighbor the terrarium enthusiast, who had his snake friend coiled around him from head to toe. He was standing there, head tilted way back, bellowing at me in outrage. But I may have misheard him: it's quite possible he wasn't yelling *elusive* but *allusive*.

That night, Melda and I couldn't sleep. We hadn't planned anything, but the same thought crossed both our minds at the same instant — it's now or never. We slipped on our quietest sneakers and festooned ourselves with headlamps that I ended up buying on sale in Tesco, a two-for-one pack for 150 crowns. We silently slunk out of the building like two reptiles and from that moment on started to communicate in kind, in a barely audible hiss. The stars were out that night . . . I can't write they were in the sky because they were all over — they sparkled in place of tires in the small parking lot, like glittering fairy lights they coiled vine-like around two streetlamps, they skidded down the slide as if Míra had flung a handful of sparks instead of mints, and they gleamed even among the dog shit on the grass in front of my window.

Piles of scrap metal littered the courtyard of the ruin across the street. Melda's eyes were definitely shining a lot brighter than the crappy flashlights from Tesco when he guesstimated under his breath how much a junkyard might pay him for all this. In a sudden premonition that painfully sliced through my body like a razor blade, I yearned to get inside, into the building, as quickly as possible. The windows and doors were covered with particleboard from this side, too, but in one we managed to find a gaping hole.

"Go ahead," I commanded, "you can do it. You're a robot."

Melda grabbed the edges of the crack and pulled them away from each other so easily and naturally as if it were an oyster that had just been served to an experienced diner in a posh restaurant.

I sensed it. The very first room we entered was the lungs. It throbbed, contracting and expanding as the building inhaled and exhaled, and we contracted along with it.

"Jesus, what is this place," Melda let out a feeble squeal, "that corner is black, this one's silver all over, but ain't nothing here! I'm going back to the courtyard."

But just then a strong exhalation flung us into another room. Judging by the color and structure, it was evidently the liver. This building was not just a heavy smoker, I thought, but an alcoholic to boot: the liver was without a doubt abnormally enlarged, and moldy leftover food from McDonald's was lying on a kitchen counter along with empty bottles of the cheapest vodka. We quickly squeezed our way out through a small hatch.

I didn't recognize the organ we found ourselves inside of next. But something completely unexpected happened: out of the blue, Melda shot out of his spot, swirled through the air, and ended up with his back plastered to a wall.

"What's this?" he whined haplessly, trying in vain to peel himself off the wall. He looked ridiculous, his limbs flailing weakly like a fly stuck to flypaper, and in that moment I truly saw him, powerless and paralyzed, in all the glorious shabbiness of his lost existence: the graying façade of a face cracked with wrinkles, thin, greasy hair, colorless fish eyes . . . I felt ashamed for the sympathy that gripped my heart, for his plastered wretchedness was indistinguishable from my own.

I tried to pry him off the wall, but that didn't work. It was magnetic, and Melda was nothing but screws —

Where was I? Here I read that the first swallows have arrived. As Doctor Gnuj said, I have to open up to the world and not gape at my alter ego plastered to the wall of the building body, I have to open up to the returning swallows.

Dawn was breaking. The sieve of the sifting pan let light through, and we were left at the bottom with now useless headlamps.

We walked up the half-crumbled staircase into the last room, the head. Three paintings were leaning against the wall. I brushed away the cobwebs with my sleeve: two still lifes, one Christ.

"We'll take the paintings, Melda, fuck the iron."

Melda and I slept through the whole next day without partaking in our usual dose of europlonk.

"I want to come back," Alice told me in a dream. She was drawing nearer to me through the building from which Melda and I had just returned, the house of the human body, and with each step she took, she grew one year younger.

"You're not getting along with Bob? You want to come back home from Costa del Sol, to the chilly and forever windy coast of disharmony? To Anděl? To I. P. Pavlova? To Modřany?"

She shook her head and rolled her eyes to let me know that I was wrong as usual, that once again I didn't get it, and that she wasn't some damn guest, our fingers were just on the point of touching, but only when she embraced me and snuggled tightly against me did I understand that she wanted to go back inside me.

"Return to my belly," I requested, "I've already got Grandma's grave in my chest."

The Fifty-first of Marchember, 2851

(1st line: Arabic letters. 2nd line: Cyrillic script. Pell-mell.)

Underneath the mattress

The trap snapped shut and firmly clamped around my memory. On February 18, 1961, my mom had wedged a book underneath my mattress to make sure I'd be sleeping on a flat surface. She forgot about it. Hanging from a long string, a monkey-shaped rattle quivered above me, and I didn't take my eyes off it for a single moment. They say the blind live in time, not space. If that's true, I was a blind person back then. All of Grandpa's clocks ticked away within my veins, and in my left hemisphere, my grandma diced apples from the garden for strudel.

Mom's friend later took the crib for her own child. She discovered the forgotten book underneath the mattress. It was Zola's *L'Assommoir*.

Book signing

I was waiting at the bus stop for the 167 going in the direction of Motol Hospital. I was looking forward to going to the two-thousand-thirty-sixth waiting room in my life, having kept a precise record ever since the days of *L'Assommoir*. This time I was to be welcomed by the surgery waiting room located on the ground floor right by the foyer. Starting New Year's Day, the government rescinded the thirty-crown fee for seeing a doctor, so now I'd be able to breathe in the cloying smell of white plaster and disinfectant free of charge. A third eye had sprouted in the middle of my forehead and it needed to be removed by a specialist. I'd given written consent to the presence of med students.

It took me a while to notice her: the girl was half-sitting, half-lying at the bus stop next to the piss-soaked wall, indifferent to the cold and her surroundings, writhing and undulating like an amoeba. Her face and arms protruding from a Microsoft T-shirt were covered in sores. Propped up against the sidewalk with one hand, she held a bread roll in the other, trying in vain to bite into it.

The passersby gave her a wide berth, young folks indistinguishable from one another rushing to get to banks and cellphone providers and brand new labs and massage salons and doctors' offices, and everybody acting as if she weren't even there — I, too, stared at her in secret so she wouldn't notice, she might think I wanted to help her eat the bread roll or that I'd rip it out of her bony hands and fling it into the distance, to the Dobrovský bookstore across the street from the bus stop where Zdeněk Svěrák's nauseatingly convivial book signing was currently taking place.

She's long past due for the morgue, I thought. The bus arrived. I wasn't the only one gawking squeamishly at this pitiful creature on the ground, and so it was with reluctance that — show's over — we all got on the bus. Some of the flowers being brought to patients turned their heads toward her, bouquets that should have belonged to her.

In another time and place this was an image of you, Alice. You're already dissolving, receding, changing, thinning, waning into the distance, and yet it's as if someone has burned the image into the back of my brain. Where am I going? Take the foot off the brake! Quick, away from these images to the stench all hospitals emit, close your eyes and breathe in deeply. And so I stepped into the restaurant of the senses that will soon be razed to the ground.

How was it still able to eat? And so, so voraciously, this body, this washed-up bag of bones . . . From what force of habit? It could be that even the dead, when the attendants turn their backs to them, trembling from the cold, in that iciness dispersed around them, furtively sink their teeth into the attendants' lunch.

2300 BC, the Ipuwer Papyrus

Right pervades the land in name, but what men do in trusting to it is Wrong. The robber is a possessor of riches; gates, columns, and walls are burned up. Indeed, chests of ebony are shattered, the laws of the council chamber are thrown out. Forget though all your strife and think only of joy until the break of day when you shall descend into the land where silence reigns.

As anger alone

Oh, if only I could shed tears and lament over your graves, brothers and sisters, whom I salute. But the murderers of the world do not bother. At least then the cries, the preconscious shrieks of the mute, breaking out of the viscera.

As anger alone can I be understood
a pulse, silence, and sentence.

Cannibalism

How many hours, months, and years have passed since my last entry? In the end I realize there is no small and large, important and trivial, personal and mythical — the dominant can no longer be distinguished from the background.

And it's a known fact that people who have spent their entire lives in a dense rainforest, where objects are never more than a few meters away, are incapable of finding their bearings in open terrain. This whole time I've been wordlessly stretching my hands out in front of me, stubbornly confident that I would touch the mountain peaks. And at other times I've spent hours and hours examining the lines on my fingers, as if they were roads on a map that would ultimately lead me to safety.

And one day during this muted time Melda disappeared, this time for good. I wander around Anděl. When women come out of the shopping mall, wearing masks over their faces and the brilliant façade of normality, I notice that some of them have machete handles sticking out of their torsos. Many of the women boldly sling their bags of spoils across them. I ask the homeless hanging around the Anděl metro station and the Na Knížecí bus station, I wander through Sacré-Coeur Park, I look at the motionless kangaroos behind the bars . . . but nobody knows anything about him.

I snoop around the ruin across the street with some hope, where the scaffolding was now, too, withering away in solidarity, I go through its lungs and liver and head. The girl in the Microsoft T-shirt is squatting in its bowels.

"Whaddaya want?" she snaps at me, as if the huge body of the building belonged to her.

"I'm looking for Melda."

"Got a smoke? Well, yes or no?"

I hand her my pack and ingratiatingly offer her my whole self. "I'm Běta."

"Don't give a rat's ass," she says, fruitlessly trying to light one, "what your name is. And piss off. This is my spot now."

I crawl out through the crack in the boarded-up window.

Back home I curl up into a cocoon, crawl into my sleeping bag, and the sound of the zipper closing shut is the same as when that white body bag zipped shut over the corpse, it sounds like a thundering avalanche that sweeps me away in an instant as if I were a box of matches. They've become damp underneath the freezing mass and are now useless. I don't have the energy to make even one lousy snow angel.

The stolen paintings are still here, propped up against a cardboard wall. A bowl of crimson apples with a pheasant. What if, I imagine, it's an overpainting of another overpainting, one painting covering another, layer by layer, just like with prehistoric paintings on cave walls? It seems to be more magic than art. I want to try to peel off the first layer at least, but I can't even budge. Loneliness has forged a bullet out of me while simultaneously turning me into the target.

Under the pretense of physical and mental ailments, I'm capable of visiting up to four doctors a day. It's warm in the waiting rooms, the gas has been cut off in my apartment, and people will often strike up a conversation with me.

"Don't I know you from somewhere?"

"Maybe from some other waiting room."

"But aren't you . . ."

"You're mistaken."

"You're the spitting image of her."

"Don't forget that recollection is always a reconstruction, never a reproduction."

"I agree. We change a story every time we retell it." A toothy grin. "It'll soon be our turn."

A sweeping gesture. Laughter. "Oh yes, before you know it, our time will come."

Most places have a coffee vending machine and a reception desk where a creature sits motionless like a torso and glittering like an aviary full of stuffed birds in a chateau park.

I've stopped eating and drinking and sleeping and my body has turned into a transparent carp scale, for Christmas is here again, and on the 23rd I manage to leave the basement and use my savings to buy a snake at an aquarium shop.

Kingsnakes of the Colubridae family are often mistaken for venomous coral snakes. Nine species have been recognized to date. Primarily nocturnal creatures, they are known for their cannibalism. They are members of the genus *Lampropeltis*, which means "clad in light."

At first I'm incapable of killing a mouse, so my snake goes hungry. But all it takes is a news report about an anti-Muslim demonstration at Prague Castle with several politicians attending to make me seize a mouse by its tail and bash it against the table. The clad-in-light soon gorges itself and dead mice are now lying all over the place. Three dogs are horsing around in a huge shipping container while Alice and Dylan's laughter echoes off the tin walls. It resonates from such a distance, a three-and-a-half hour flight on a Boeing 737, and still I feel its blade stabbing into my stomach and fear the door will open to reveal my smiley daughter, and one look around will be enough for her to grasp the desolation, the revolting tableau of little mouse carcasses her mother is wallowing in, hell-bent on getting bitten. With every swallow the snake takes, a helicopter thunders above me, landing at Na Homolce Hospital, and it thunders while circling over Rouffignac Cave — my womb — and the mammoth on its wall trembles and goes extinct.

A horizontal fall

. . . to abandon my life, that horizontal fall, and intently watch it disappear along with water down the drain, vanishing in the underground of Prague, my city, to commence merely a vapid reproduction of daily news. The temptation is strong, because this clinging weariness wraps around me and suffocates me like shrink-wrap.

Still, a three-by-three centimeter hole would have to be drilled into each medium to let my snake slip into them at any time.

January 19, 2015

Paris is a sad sight. Tourism plummets after terrorist attacks.

January 19 is considered the most depressing day of the year.

The shrunken breast of an old woman wheezily reminisced.

The Nazi

arrives around four, five o'clock in the afternoon, hangs around until about seven, and then at night, reigns.

We sit on chairs across from each other in the gloom of a completely empty space. The man has a black briefcase resting on his lap. His face is blank like the moon, while the moon head outside the window has his features.

The man slowly opens the briefcase. Chrome steel flashes in the dark. I know it's torture instruments. With a dispassionate, tired expression on his face, the uniformed man pulls out one of the instruments and holds it to my throat. "We'll start with the tonsils," he sighs.

I wake up. I light a cigarette and begin to tremble in the dark, the innocent color of cocoa. "Just you wait," I whisper, I hiss into the darkness until the Nazi starts to dissolve, to crumble, to disintegrate into negatively charged particles of matter. "History will cut you down. History and my snake."

That familiar, yet always new, fear: something is happening. Something's in the air. Something isn't right.

And from the Prague sewers, Mozart's *Requiem* casually rises up toward the wires.

January 21, 2015

A University of Liverpool research team has deciphered the genome of the bowhead whale having a 200-year lifespan.

Driving ban goes into effect for Russians exhibiting the sexual deviancy of fetishism, exhibitionism, and S/M.

More than half the Russian population has a favorable opinion of Joseph Stalin's role in Russian history.

Thirteen boys shot dead by ISIS extremists in the northern Iraqi city of Mosul for violating the ban on watching soccer.

The plastic bag ripped.

The needle disappeared in the fabric.

Near and far, the last leaf in Prague fell to the ground.

And if someone were to press an ear to the windowpane in the Greenland town of Nye-Sukkertoppen, they'd be able to hear a strange lullaby:

Hush, shut your eyes, little baby,
try to go to bed,
or you'll catch a bout of rabies
and then you'll be dead.

Imprint

The man in front of the door leading to the MRI had, at 10:32 a.m., a snowflake on one coat lapel and a drop of blood on the other. He hunched forward, bringing the lapels together. "I like to hope," he mumbled into his fist before entering, "that some energy impression is left in the universe after we're gone, some sort of personal imprint."

Two empty squares

Nobody's in Doctor Gnuj's waiting room. Wet snow hesitantly flutters outside the window. A hairy goblin in a fashionable winter zip-up ensemble yelps, runs off, and vanishes. I run my finger across the top of the piano. Psychiatrists clearly never dust. In my pocket, I crush a new pill vial in my fist, a pill container with a screw cap, I crush it into particles invisible to the naked eye, for both the minuscule and the immense are impossible to see.

"Well, come on in," the doctor peals out as soon as I appear in the doorway.

"Why don't you ever dust?" I dispense with a hello. "You could hire me as a cleaning lady."

I hardly have time to mull over the fleeting idea before Doctor Gnuj hollers once more, "Joyful news! The Gospel according to Gnuj!"

Only now do I notice that the heads of Freud and Jung on the wall are larger-than-life while Doctor Gnuj's is small to an astonishing degree, tiny even, despite bursting with serotonin.

Gnuj is contentedly teetering on his office chair, farther and farther, until he quite suddenly topples over chair and all to the floor. I'm shocked. First Freud and Jung's beards vanish, then their heads become angular, until finally I see in the frames two completely empty squares. My psychiatrist remains lying on his back, unperturbed, the wheels of his chair jutting toward the ceiling, and carries on as if nothing has happened: "Simply great news. I've finally got it, I figured it out. Med school wasn't a waste of time after all! No point in false modesty. Considering your twenty-one hospitalizations in the past three years, you'll apply for a disability pension and bam! — your worries are over. And now, goodbye!"

He's evidently taken a liking to this unusual position and nestles down for a nap.

"But what about my anti-depressants?" I ask in dismay. "I'm talking about Anafranil, Valdoxan, Prozac, Lamotrigine, and Mirzaten? I'm running low! Take a look yourself." I shove the atoms that used to constitute my pill vial under his nose.

He spits on my hand. I step back. "Really now, Doctor, what are you doing?"

"I spat on your hand. Now don't be shy, go ahead and take it, no prescription needed. No side effects. Every so often, when I'm in this position, serotonin trickles down from my brain into my mouth."

Melda winks at me from one of the empty squares that had been Freud. "You're a sieve, Běta, just a sieve merely sifting through other people's identities."

I leave the doctor's office. By now a bunch of people have gathered around the piano, folks of different races and nationalities. They communicate with each other in a language I don't understand in the slightest. That it seems to be Czech astonishes me. Even though the sky is sprawled across the rooftops, it's stopped snowing. I almost trip over the dolled-up pooch. Is it really a dog? I see paws, a muzzle, a tail, an ear . . . but the whole of the dog escapes me. This frightens me: what if this disintegration into prime elements, this fragmentation into particulars, is also true for other phenomena, and reality will churn before my eyes in an incomprehensible muddle?

I pass the window display of a travel agency. I freeze. "Cheap accommodation in the resort town of Nerja on the Costa del Sol." Do they mean huge shipping containers? And I immediately hear Alice's whisper, right in my ear: "Remember, Mom? That one time when we walked through the village of Újezd pod Troskami and the gravel beneath my shoes burst into laughter. I wanted to make it laugh one more time but you said no. I was suddenly shrouded in a silence heavy as Grandma's quilt soaked in water and thick like the semolina porridge I hate —"

Míra and Bobeš are dragging a bobsled across the gravel in front of the building — the snow melting straightaway — across the gravel that hasn't laughed in a long time. I barely respond to their hello. I'm in a hurry. The room has an incredibly sour stench, the remnants of wine evaporating from the cartons. I waste no time in sinking my nails into the partridge (or whatever it is) in the painting and violently strip off the first layer until blood spurts out.

Out of the frying pan into the fire

And once, it was at our cottage, I yanked the doll out of your hands, opened the stove, and stuffed it headfirst into the flames, with Ken. Its hair emitted a soft, Christmassy crackle, and you kept howling and screaming exactly as if someone had thrown your doll into the fire. It was only later that I realized coating the Barbie in flour, egg, and breadcrumbs and deep-frying it slowly until golden brown would have been much more satisfying.

Another time, after one of your innocent peccadilloes, I packed your little backpack, shoved you out of the door into the hallway, and said goodbye to you with heartfelt, motherly words: "Off to the orphanage with you and don't ever come back."

And then —

Analytical thinking

I ran into my former boss today on National Avenue in front of the Academy of Sciences, the one who had laid me off a while back. He was dressed head to toe in hockey gear — a Bauman helmet, jersey, shin guards, elbow pads, jockstrap, socks — and was teetering on his skates in front of me.

"Bauers?" I inquired with a conspiratorial wink.

"How'd you know?" he beamed. "How've you been all this time?"

I beamed back, "Fantastic! Imagine that yesterday, for one billionth of a second, nobody in the entire world died." Although I did eye him a bit skeptically, no way was this a dream. "Going from or to a game?"

"Me . . ." he sighed almost existentially, "nowadays, all I do is go . . . from game to game."

A small crowd started to form around us. Drivers honked their horns. We could hear *The Rite of Spring* raining down on us from the National Theater. Thanks to some daring drama- turgy, ballerinas danced on a gas burner as though their lives depended on it.

Just then a scientist stepped out of the Academy of Sciences. The mob parted. "The Crowd," flashed through my mind, it's like in that short story "The Crowd" by Ray Bradbury where the exact same people would show up in different parts of the city whenever an accident occurred.

"Silence, please!" The scientist commanded respect, only my boss ignored him.

"I opened a bookstore for hockey players, but nobody's come by so far. I don't get it. Jágr popped in once, but he didn't buy anything."

The last whining words fizzled out in the silence. The scientist shushed us and started to talk. "We've just received a report from the board of experts working for the American *Bulletin of the Atomic Scientists* that the world is nearing its end."

A kid started to bawl and the hockey gear rattled in disagreement. *The Rite of Spring* subsided and the legless ballerinas bowed their torsos.

"Personally, I have to agree. The general term for mutually connected structures, the rudiments that give rise to a hierarchy of subordination and a structure of causality, is known as *the system*."

One of my boss's skate blades got lodged in a crack between paving stones. He froze like a golem and began to pry it out.

"Even you," the scientist turned to him with aversion, "are a system of sorts."

"I disagree," the thin voice of a ballerina's torso spoke up from the back, "logical statements, as we know, fall under six categories: the definition of a problem, the hypothesis stipulating a ca . . ."

"Shut up, bitch!" The hockey player's patience was exhausted.

". . . cause!" the slim woman finished boldly, but my boss had already lifted his hockey stick and suddenly smacked the scientist across his back.

The dumpster lid creaked.

Alice aimed her headlamp inside.

Just that single beam of light, otherwise darkness.

The crowd was getting worked up and began to chant: "From game to game! From game to game!"

Some backed the athlete, and they were by far larger in number, others had the scientist's back. I thought he would give it up and slink back into the safety of the Academy, but he surprisingly brandished his tablet like a shield and swiftly applied analytical thinking to turn his fist into beveled flint. "The days of breakneck slaloming between glass retorts in my youth will finally come in handy!" and a lunge of flint followed. My boss wanted to step back, but the blade of his skate stuck between paving stones held him back. Like a lunatic, he started to wildly thrash his hockey stick, also a Bauer, around himself.

The dumpster lid creaked.

Alice aimed her headlamp inside.

Just that single beam of light, otherwise darkness.

Three dogs were running around her legs.

"Each retort I zipped by" — flint struck the shin guard — "cracked and crashed behind my back," at that moment the scientist broke the hockey stick in two with a mighty blow, "the condensed vapor of evaporated liquid rippled through the air and vanished in an instant."

"I saw Jágr with my own eyes, dumbass!" the athlete sobbed and sunk to his knees.

The gawkers slowly began to disperse. Some headed to Café Slavia for way overpriced coffee, some took a tram without paying the fare to I. P. Pavlov Square to grab lunch at KFC. One poor wretch, stuck in a fissure of time like the hockey player's skate, even went next door to Viola for a poetry reading.

The dumpster lid creaked.

Alice aimed her headlamp inside.

Just that single beam of light, otherwise darkness.

Three dogs were running around her legs.

They were Ibizan Hounds.

On National Avenue.

He popped in once.

Silence, please.

From game to game.

Analytical thinking.

Causes.

Glass retorts.

End of the world.

The dumpster lid creaked. Alice aimed her headlamp inside. Just that single beam of light, otherwise darkness. Three dogs were running around her legs. They were Ibizan Hounds, a Spanish breed of dog found nowhere else in Europe.

Inside the dumpster, Alice found a laptop manual in Chinese, a fresh smoked ham, a block of Gouda cheese, an unopened bottle of whiskey, silence, causes, and retorts. Just as she was about to shut the lid and leave, she noticed a pale torso at the bottom. She leaned in as far as she could and reached out her hand toward the illuminated spot.

"But this is . . ." she whispered in astonishment, "my old Barbie doll. Her hair is still singed."

Ready to break,

the wave strangely and suddenly becomes immobile, as if it has frozen stiff, as if it were trying to shinny up a sunbeam into the sky, even the surfer on its frozen crest raises his hands and turns into a statue. A sandcastle on the distant shore slowly, and unnoticed, melts into the beach.

At 7:30 in the Siberian town of Gorno-Altaysk, a Yevgeniy hitched his horse to a wagon full of furniture and motley junk. Nobody, not even himself, knew where he was going. Yet in the cottage he was leaving behind, lying in the closet next to the skeletons, was a tiny map the size of a ruble, marking his destination with an Orthodox cross.

New Year's Eve, December 31, 2014

And in the span of one second the morphology of duration and evanescence on my snake's back transformed. I wondered if myth could survive impact with reality. My snake was sniffling and coughing. I pressed a forehead thermometer to its flat head — and turned white as a sheet. Even though the temperature of snakes depends on the surrounding temperature, my snake was burning up. I coiled him into a basket and headed to the vet.

Foreigners with earmuffs surged through Prague, and many a tourist would immediately go up in flames if a match were struck next to their mouths. Spectacular fireworks were still slumbering in their cannons.

"Get a move on," my snake said, "I feel like crap."

I smoothed out the blanket in the basket and broke into a run, but fearing for the fragile cargo and going against the human streams coming at me kept the pace slow.

A car stopped next to the curb. "Hey, Auntie! Where are you partying tonight? You look like Little Red Riding Hood." My niece. Right on time. And yes: I did have on a red jacket and basket hooked on my elbow.

"So where are you partying tonight?"

"At the vet's."

"Don't let it get you down. I'll be at *The Rite of Spring*."

"Gas burners?"

"You bet. Gas burners."

The waiting room was indescribable chaos. In the narrow aisle between benches, Agama, Anaconda, and Alfie were crowded together, if I were to limit myself to just the first letter of the Alphabet. Some of the animals were already drunk, welcoming each new firecracker with a round of oinks, barks, hisses, and honks. Many of them grabbed each other by the paws and attempted to dance a roundelay. Maybe it was a sense of dread, but nobody was coming out of the vet's office. Until, finally — "Next!"

Well? No reaction from anyone. I was quick to take advantage and slipped inside. The vet was busy arguing with the nurse and ignored us. I overheard him say, "How many times do I have to tell you, colors are not external, they're contrived by the brain." I instinctively looked out the window. In that instant, red, green, and yellow lit up the darkness, fireworks created by my mind.

At that moment I noticed with dread the Nazi's black briefcase lying on the examination table.

"Ma'am, please don't interrupt, insurance doesn't cover snakes anyhow. So take this and off you go."

I gripped the broad-spectrum Augmentin antibiotics in my hand and quickly backed away. A domesticated Pig, Pelican, and Peacock all started to Push their way into the open door, and then it happened: the astronomical clock and all the bells of the world began to strike midnight. The animals stiffened as if they'd all croaked. This cued the snake to stick its head out of the basket, throw off the blanket, and get ready to launch into its New Year's speech. All of a sudden though, and poorly timed at that, the air boomed with Ryba's Christmas Mass chorale, and yet I could still make out the rather thin voices under these notes. While the animals were struck dumb, while the colors faded, the fish had rediscovered their speech, lost in the Pleistocene.

February 1, 2015

Mom was complaining yesterday that her gums ached. Today, on her ninety-first birthday, she collapsed to the floor and couldn't get up. She called me, me and Nadia. Her cellphone is kept on a string around her neck. "I'm on my way." I'm on my way, Mom, as soon as I kill a few mice.

I missed the bus. I missed the tram. "Don't die," I implored the ticket inspector, "not yet. We're not ready yet."

In the cardiology ward at Motol Hospital, the doctor told me, "Say goodbye to your mother. Untreated heart attack."

We were all gathered here except for Alice and Dylan, ten of us altogether. The doctor had eyes the color of the heavens, I guess so I would more easily come to terms with it.

I called Alice. "Your grandma's dying."

"I know," she calmly replied.

I blew up at her. "How could you possibly know this?"

"You wouldn't understand. It would only make you angry. Hang in there, Mom." And she hung up.

"Death is a mere part of hard life," Nadia said. "I brought Wolker, Hora, and Sova. Mom liked, likes them a lot. We'll recite their poems to her."

My God. All the relatives assumed their positions around the bed, I felt like one of the menhirs at Stonehenge. Mom's eyes were closed and her skin had that terrible yellow-green hue, the hue of the dead.

"It's a matter of hours," the doctor quietly said and disappeared.

The blanket rose and fell at irregular intervals. In the neighboring bed, behind the divider, a man was singing *Carmen*.

"That's *Carmen*, Don José's part, second act," Nadia said. Mom imperceptibly moved her head, as though she were nodding in agreement. The ending of the aria was drowned out by Kryštof's wailing. I made myself heard over him. "Mom, the assessment of my disability status came today. After evaluating the state of my health the social security office has arrived at a favorable factual determination! I have been deemed incapable of retaining permanent gainful employment and should only work in jobs that place no undue burden on my physical, sensory, and mental faculties."

God knows why the word "Versatil" popped into my mind as I finished bragging.

Kryštof, pacified by the nurse in white and the myriad of serpentine vines surrounding Mom, had calmed down and placed his hairless monkey toy under his dying great-grandmother's chin. Nadia leafed through the poetry.

"Not Wolker," I pleaded.

Time, brother to my heart, who goes
and measures out the hours of my doom,
hesitates, collapses into my face,
dozes off and fills the air with the scent of bloom.

I went to find the doctor. The sound of gunshots was coming from the computer.

"I'd like to stay here overnight."

His face immediately turned into a mask of understanding. "Sorry, but we cannot do that."

"In that case we'll take my mom home."

I held onto the hope that he'd expand his repertoire, but nothing doing. "Sorry, we cannot do that either."

The stone didn't budge, a thousand slaves didn't shift it a single millimeter.

"You have to understand, we want to be . . . with her . . . now that . . ."

One nurse told another, "I'm gonna go change the bandages in room three."

I missed the bus. I missed the tram. The Versatil drove into my vein. I didn't go back to my basement apartment but to the girl in the ruin. "My mom's dying. Want a bread roll?"

She snatched it out of my hand and bit into it greedily. I looked around: no guts, no lungs, no liver — just a layer of plaster on a cement floor, just boarded-up windows, just a layer of plaster on the girl's sores, just her eyes boarded up.

I went to Mickey D's and had a double burger.

February 2, 2015

A couple of folks in bathrobes and a couple of bums were sitting in the foyer of Motol Hospital. Out of habit I asked them about Melda. I had noticed yesterday that one of the paintings was missing. The one with the athletic body of Jesus Christ. Without the thieves.

Ah, Melda, where in the world is that giant magnet that has drawn you in with its mighty force?

"Oh, that guy, said he was flying to Spain," said the chest-length beard and blackened jacket, Adidas surprisingly. He was making it up. All bums lie. Just for the hell of it, life is more bearable that way.

A hairdresser's was also located in the lobby. I'll stop by on my way out. Sharp scissors, hot fan. A new dye, a new chic hairdo, just like Melda wanted. Crackling hair. An urn. Associations are formed in the frontal cerebral cortex. I took the elevator to the third floor and my heart was beating like crazy. Two doctors, conversing together in diagnoses rather than sentences, had to be able to hear it. I didn't have the courage to ring the buzzer. A lady with a bag full of clementines did it for me. "Don't worry, he was singing *Carmen* yesterday," I said.

Mom was sitting in bed, leafing through a tabloid. "Well, what took you so long? Did you hear that Leoš Mareš is dealing with his first breakup of the year with Faltýnová?"

The doctor. Excitedly, in a half-whisper. "We couldn't believe it, but there you have it." He shrugged his shoulders and walked off.

I wondered, Alice, did you know about this, too? The smell of clementines wafted through the room, and while peels the color of Buddhist robes and garbageman vests fell to the ground, the waves with surfers on their crests again turned to stone.

Prague

reflects off the river. And so it is here twofold — reality and its reflection — while I can barely endure the one. Awareness clings to everything, the river, the skyline of Hradčany, Jánský vršek Street where I used to visit Aunt Kozlová when I was a kid, and to my own words. Awareness, and yet a remarkable emptiness, for all these props — and even my speech is a prop — are just an accretion of completely empty squares.

My brother Igor

was an architect. He designed houses that nobody wanted to build. He'd wander Prague for hours and stand in front of vacant lots, imagining his designs coming to life.

One March day in 1984, as he stood in front of his drawing board, he felt a sudden, sharp pain in his chest and couldn't breathe. His coworkers called an ambulance, thinking he was having a heart attack. It wasn't a heart attack but a panic attack. From Motol they transferred him to the Bohnice Psychiatric Hospital, to dreaded Pavilion No. 26. There were ten patients to a room and the only thing they had in common was the way they clutched their bags to their chests all day in fear of others stealing anything.

An attendant walked them through the grounds. Not even then did the loonies stop pressing their backpacks to their chests. And then Igor got his first free leisure time. He was supposed to report to the central therapy building to weave a basket that in the future his sister would use for carrying snakes.

He wrapped a rope round his ankle, tied a stone to it, and slowly walked into the Vltava. Back then Mom told me, and she never claimed otherwise, that he had hanged himself in our cottage. God knows why one rope seemed more bearable to her than the other.

Caprichos

I wiped up the blood and wrung it out into the bucket. Murder also required swift action on my part. In the painting beneath the layer with the partridge, an abstraction now appeared that resembled the famous DNA double helix. Ever since my snake had spoken, each and every word froze inside me, and not even the fact that the deepest structures of our brains were identical to reptile brains could restore my speech.

I headed to The Depths. I was barely hobbling along, Igor's boulder tied to my leg.

The pub was totally empty. One music video followed another on a giant screen.

"Do you want the classic?"

What is she asking me exactly? If I want Mozart instead of Lady Gaga?

"I mean the sirloin in cream sauce," the waitress explained to me kindly.

If only he were to walk in now, that person I'd gotten drunk with so quickly and efficiently all those years ago who'd then urinated in empty Lidická Street on the colossal tracks of the tank, until war broke out.

I watched the waitress closely as she stood behind the bar by the gurgling coffee machine. She was coated in a bloom, a frost blurring her features. Suddenly, a small hard black light hit me right between the eyes like a puck.

"Mind if I sit here?"

"Why here? The place is empty. I'm not afraid of getting old."

"Sorry?"

"We've met before."

"I don't recall. I'm from Brno."

"I don't give a damn. You could be from Nye-Sukkertoppen in Greenland or Gorno-Altaysk in Siberia for all I care, what difference does it make."

"To be free at least for a single day," he sighed, "of one's frontal lobes, where boundaries, inhibitions, reason, and the consciousness of responsibilities reside."

The waitress brought me the sirloin. I slid it over to the man. "All and all, I don't actually have any responsibilities, come to think of it."

He dug into the food with relish. I stared attentively at his moving jaws. I tried to concentrate on every contortion of his face, discover every feature and expression, but what I actually saw astounded me: just an arm, a leg, a tooth, a hair . . . Like the dog before, the man, too, had disintegrated into particulars I simply couldn't make cohere and see as a whole. So not even he is "external" but has been born and died in my mind. The waitress, the man, and me. I gave up. I could see myself, sitting across from me, like Prague mirrored in the Vltava, and so the only thing I saw was my upside-down reflection.

My phone rang. Alice. "Mom, I went to Madrid with Dylan!"

"Did you go to see the El Grecos and Goyas in the Prado?"

"Mom, no, we went to a protest! The March for Change organized by the left-wing Podemos Party. Pablo Iglesias shook my hand! They've ended the austerity measures. Aren't you following the news?"

Yes, Picasso's *Guernica* was there, too. What would I see when I peeled off another layer?

I didn't even notice the man had finished eating and left. I pulled out a broken light bulb from my purse, held it right in front of my eyes, and gazed at the snapped filament for a long time. It contained the entire world — reptiles, brains, black pucks, ropes, dumpsters, Madrid streets full of people, blood-soaked rags, El Greco, and Goya.

And then a weird, faintly familiar noise from the basement. It was night planing smooth nothingness.

February 1, 2015, Sunday

The March for Change kicked off in Madrid at high noon at Cibeles Square and moved toward the historical center. After a successful election, the leftist Prime Minister of Greece, Alexis Tsipras, declared the five years of austerity that had caused humiliation and suffering were now over. "People are sick and tired of it," Antonia Fernández told Reuters. "Ninety percent of the wealth of this planet is owned by one percent of the population."

In 1823, Francesco Goya covered the walls of two rooms in his Quinta del Sordo estate, the Villa of the Deaf, with black paintings. Scientists believe his loss of hearing may have been caused by the lead contained in the paints he used.

The filament continued to quiver.

Beneath the double helix,

something was written in French on the painting. I rang my neighbor's doorbell. He lit up like a Christmas tree. "Is it time?"

It took me a minute before I realized what he was talking about: a month back, we'd agreed to mate our kingsnakes. He had a male and I a female.

"Could you do me a favor and translate something for me from French?"

"The same spot viewed from a different angle," he read slowly, but surely, "offers a subject of the utmost interest. It is so varied that I think I could keep busy for months without changing my place, simply turning now to the right and now to the left . . ."

"Is the author of the quote given?"

"Cézanne. Looks like we'll have to hold off on the mating till spring."

"What? All right. Have you given any thought to what we'll do with thirty snake eggs if it works?"

"I could keep busy for months . . . simply turning now to the right and now to the left . . ."

"Thirty small clad-in-lights?"

We were standing in the hallway by the mailboxes with the flaps of the Prague 5 magazine sticking out of them. Kindergarten registration fast approaching! During the excursion there was still time for a joint prayer. Make the most of your maternity leave and become an aerobics instructor! The homeless received clothes and blankets as well as a food package of goulash and bread.

"Not yet," I told my neighbor, "I'm not ready to peel off the next layer yet."

To keep from losing my edge, I sunk my vulture claws into the wine boxes. It was hard as hell, but I didn't give up. To get rid of Melda once and for all.

Once one wall was bare and I had to wade through cardboard everywhere, I sat down in the debris on the floor and again thumbed through *Your Prague Five*, the monthly bulletin for the district's residents. A photograph accompanied an article about the homeless. I froze and brought it closer to my eyes like a snapped filament, like my own strand of hair harboring my DNA, like a snowflake I'm panicked will vanish before I'm able to see it. The photo was of a line of people winding toward a pot of goulash, and in the line stood Melda.

"There'll be no trace of you left anyhow," I hissed, "nothing at all, just a pile of rusted screws."

Ashram

It was a little like an apocalyptic movie: volcanoes spewing magma, mountains crumbling to the ground, which itself was splitting open. And yet there was this one unfathomable difference: people kept living their everyday lives as if nothing were happening. Sometimes the chasm would swallow a person or a city, but everyone else paid it no mind. What's going on in Spain? In Greenland? Siberia? Do these labels still carry any meaning? The news tells me nothing, as usual. It's made me go completely sour, I have a lemon inside my head instead of a brain, like my lost companion.

I step out of my basement dwelling straight into an ashram. Some guru is concentrating on biting his fingernails.

"Could you do me a favor and tell me what's going on?"

"The Ouroboros serpent has wrapped itself around the Earth's crust and bitten into its own tail in Mongolia near the city of Choibalsan."

As soon as he said this, the ground beneath his lotus-positioned legs opened up and the man plummeted down, still nibbling on his fingernails. I knew what he'd said was true. The particle accelerator near Geneva also had just fallen into the depths as the serpent squeezed the Earth tighter and tighter, finally crushing it completely. So it then started to devour itself. Before long, nothing remained of the serpent. The right angles of a square pierced interstellar space. I swirled in it, covered in the ubiquitous snake scales, my feet moaning and wailing because there was nowhere for them to stand.

"Běda, open your eyes!"

Self-destruction and self-restoration. Dream devoured dream.

Colors

An overlooked and paradoxical difference between the totalitarian period and today is that back then nobody locked building doors in Prague, whereas now you can't get in anywhere without a key. All you had to do before was enter inconspicuously, walk up the stairs to the attic, and pull yourself through a dormer window onto the roof, where you would suddenly find yourself with a bird's eye view, in the skin of an entirely different world.

I was bringing Aunt Kozlová a hundred crowns from Mom. My aunt was broke and had a hysterical fear of one color combination — blue and green.

"Thank you very much, Bětuška, I'll spend fifty on rum and give the other fifty to the Infant Jesus on Karmelitská Street."

On my way down to Malá Strana Square I tried my luck and pushed on a gate on Vlašská Street. It opened a crack. I slipped inside. Laundry was drying on the courtyard balcony. Green and blue towels, blue and green tablecloths. It smelled of beef broth and shoe polish. If someone were to ask me what I was doing here, I'd say I was looking for Štěpánka Kočí.

I went up the stairs, and my heart behind my ribs beat with anticipation, alert like an animal. Maybe the attic would be locked, maybe the dormer would be too small. Clotheslines spanned the attic, too. A broken-down spin dryer speckled with pigeon droppings, cracked roof tiles, a wardrobe resembling a pudgy old woman. In no time I was on the roof. I felt a pang in my eyes as they were jabbed by the spires and rooftops within reach, that domesticated clad-in-light, venom-free, I reached for a cloud and shoved it under my sweater. An overlooked and paradoxical difference. It's my secret, one I'd never tell anyone. Petřín had my back. I scattered my lunch to the pigeons.

amygdala and hippocampus suffer from bipolar disorder."

I looked out the window. The No. 17 was rattling its way toward Výstaviště. Perhaps a black Mercedes was slowly cruising by, its driver picking out the next augur from the men hanging around there. The steep steps leading up to Letná were being ascended by people with a diencephalon, midbrain, and medulla oblongata. It began to snow. Snowflakes fell on the pons Varolii, which harbors the center for basic unconditioned reflexes.

Tomorrow hesitantly opened to me like a closet with its skeletons.

The balcony of Europe

And one day, a day drifting in on the tide like your little boat carved out of bark, a day swept along from God knows where by a gust of time to arrive here, it's August again. Prague is ablaze, and only the Old Town cobblestones conceal any vestige of coolness. I stand in the restroom of the Václav Havel Airport and hold my wrists under the stream of cold water for a long time. I'm not in a hurry, I've got time. In three-and-a-half hours — I smile at myself in the mirror, at a stranger and a cleaning lady with her mop and cart full of cleaning products — in three-and-a-half hours, I'll be able to hug you. I can't believe it. Grinning like an idiot, my smile doesn't leave my face for a single moment.

Seated in the Boeing 737, I glimpse the outline of the wing, and when I peek out of the window, I can see all the glowing lights of my city. They run beneath me at right angles and yet somehow remain round. I think I could keep busy for months without changing my place, simply turning now to the right and now to the left — for a moment, I catch a glimpse of a man below, lying motionless on a bench. I stay calm: I've known for a long time now that it's not Andrei, your father.

I must have fallen asleep for a moment because an unbroken layer of snow has covered the ground from Prague to Costa del Sol, disrupted only by a stretch of snow angels winding from here to there, the imprints of our flapping bodies. The thirsty spring earth doesn't worry me because I'm sure the thaw will never come and our wings will remain here forever.

We wait for the luggage; I take the suitcases wrapped in plastic that remind me of nothing at all, and set them obligingly in front of my fellow humans. I love them all, I even pat the head of the impossibly whiny little girl who squealed behind me the entire flight and ran her little airplane through my hair. And then it happens. Out of the blue, a sharp as yet unexperienced pain shoots through me from hemispheres to toes with no fore-warning. Something similar must've happened to Lot's wife, I think at once, as my whole body stiffens and turns to stone, with someone else's suitcase in my hand. "May I?" "Of course."

The little girl must've noticed my transformation because she starts to dance wildly in circles around me as if I were a plague column. I use my remaining strength to spit in her face, "Better watch out, you brat, I'm a Kikimora." All of a sudden, instead of suitcases an assortment of strange items begins to appear on the baggage carousel, things no one claims as their own: kelp and stones, teeth and claws and beaks, roots and branches and huge nests and finally human skeletons, skeletons in installments, skulls and pelvic bones, tons of human bones from death camps, circling round and round, and nobody wants them, everyone goes their separate ways, as if these weren't the bones of their dead, as if they no longer acknowledge their dead, as if they've disowned them, it's just me stuck standing here, rooted to the marble, certain the other shoe will drop at any moment.

And indeed — with a single chop someone cleaves me from head to toe clean in two. Heart attack or Igor's panic attack, the symptoms are basically identical. I stagger off to the arrivals hall with my backpack that finally showed up on the carousel, though it's only one half of me that does so, having been filleted by a machete of pain. My other half curls up on the carousel belt and soon vanishes into the bowels.

It hurts like hell when Alice hugs me, touching my guts exposed by the gash. I clench my teeth and realize I'll never again be reunited with the other half of my being, that it has disappeared for good and I'll never be whole again.

I stagger along the seashore for a week, and while it's hot in Prague, there's no word to describe the swelter prevailing here. Everything quivers, flickers, vibrates in the air — one of the hounds loyally trails behind me with lolling tongue. While Alice can see, I cannot through the shroud of sweat. She doesn't ask any questions. A couple of times I go with them to do some recycling, dumpster diving, but it's hard to do with just half a body.

In Nerja we stand on the balcony of Europe with a view of Africa. I look at Africa with just one eye, and Alice can tell.

"Right pervades the land in name, but what men do in trusting to it is Wrong. The robber is a possessor of riches; gates, columns, and walls are burned up" — the Ipuwer Papyrus, 2300 BC. A leg, an arm, half a face. I lie in the ocean, I rarely leave it, children scream and jump from a high cliff and I think about whether I'll be able to get out of the ocean alive, whether

I'll ever be whole again, whether Spain also has white body bags, and whether, from here to there, at least a stem.

I hold one wrist under the stream of cold water in the restroom of the Václav Havel Airport. I don't have the guts to look in the mirror. It's raining, the water coming down in buckets. It's gotten colder. Suitcase wheels clatter on the pavement, taxi drivers on their smoke break huddle together. I'm not in a hurry. I've got time.

The riverboat *Socrates* berthed between the Palacký and Jirásek bridges, within view of the Dancing House, is both too minuscule and too immense for me to see.

January 27, 2015

Seventy years ago, the Red Army liberated the Auschwitz concentration camp where Nazis had murdered over one million people: 960,000 Jews, 75,000 Poles, 21,000 Roma, 15,000 Soviet POWs, 15,000 Czechs, Slovaks, Germans, Austrians, Ukrainians, French, Yugoslavians. In April 1947, Rudolf Höss, the commandant of the liberated camp, was sentenced to death and hanged symbolically in front of the crematorium of Auschwitz I.

Don't miss out! A tour of Auschwitz, a two-day trip for two, 46% off.

The psyche

I grasp the doorknob of time, push on the doors on Zborovská Street, and make my way around Arbes Square, but they're all locked except for the glass entries to banks.

For some strange reason, guests tend to make themselves so at home at my place they never leave. Or is that me from them?

I sit by my mom's side and read to her from whatever I

happen to grab from the bookcase. Nadia and I bought her an adjustable bed, and no need to pad it with *L'Assommoir* or Freud or Jung, it resembles a sailing ship ready to explore new, uncharted lands.

The psyche pre-existent to consciousness (e.g., in a child) partici-pates in the maternal psyche on the one hand, while on the other it reaches across to the daughter psyche. We could therefore say that every mother contains her daughter in herself and every daughter her mother, and that every woman extends backwards into her mother and forwards into her daughter. This participation and intermingling give rise to that peculiar uncertainty as regards time: a woman lives earlier as a mother, later as a daughter. The conscious experience of these ties produces the feeling that her life is spread out over genera-tions — the first step towards the immediate experience and conviction of being outside time, which brings with it a feeling of immortality.

And so I read and read and read aloud and change Mom's diapers, as she once did for me and I for you.

Over the rooftops

I was in a rush to meet Nadia at the Czech Museum of Music. I stepped into the Vltava from Children's Island, the one we always used to call Jew Island, and broke into a run across the water's surface to take a shortcut. Child's play — I couldn't understand why Jesus's disciples were so in awe of it and why I hadn't thought of getting around Prague like this sooner.

Somewhere in the depths below our brother Igor was futilely trying to ascend, trapped at the bottom by a weight, our brother, waterlogged monstrously into larger-than-life proportions, waiting to be found, fished out, and identified by the river police.

Prague reflected in the river and I, quietly gliding farther, trod its rooftops rippling in the light. The arches of a bridge stretched out above me, the barely audible echo throwing the sweet sound of my sploshing gait back at me. I flew through a flock of swans as if one of them, passed by the Sova's Mills, and glided over the weir like a water skier.

The knight beneath Charles Bridge lowered his sword, mumbling something: he was memorizing some forgotten poetry. I had to walk on my own two feet the rest of the way.

Nineteen foundation stones shifted in the subterranean belly of the National Theater.

...And the drunkards begin to dance

Běta sat in a room the size of a gym and didn't understand where she was or how she'd gotten there. Wooden benches spanned the room, a few people lay on them, covered with threadbare fur coats and torn rags. A Club stove glowed in the corner. The attendant in blue uniform walked in and dumped a shovelful of coal into it. They had the same exact stove at home, just a lot smaller.

"Where are we?" she asked Nadia, but her sister said nothing. She was chewing on a buttered slice of bread.

They both had on ugly, rumpled tights and gloves. Nadia's were all smeared with butter.

"One day, on December 21, 2011, I'll buy a pair of gloves like these for the woman who sells *Nový prostor* at Anděl." The space did not belong to Běta, and neither did the ideas taking form there.

Two framed paintings hung on the wall. Maybe she'd be able to figure out where she was from what they depicted — but even when she stood on her tiptoes, they were too high up for her to see them.

"We're in the waiting room," Nadia said, "waiting for a train. We're going to Majdalena to visit Grandma and Grandpa. Their hayloft beam fell. A woodworm ate right through it."

They went out to the front of the train station. It was freezing. Prague-Bubeneč. The trains never stopped here, just passed through.

"I forgot something inside," Běta lied and ran back into the waiting room. She took a chair and stepped on it. Now she could see the paintings clearly. The DNA double helix was in one of them and a diagram of the brain in the other. The voice coming out of the loudspeaker was unintelligible, and the dispatcher stood with his back to the trains. Trains heading to the left had the crib with *L'Assommoir* as their destination, trains heading to the right ended in the Prado in Madrid in front of Goya's painting *Saturn Devouring His Son*. The past and the future, the small and the large, the dominant and the background — all merged into one in that moment at Bubeneč Station.

The medulla oblongata, the thalamus, the subthalamus. Alice pried herself out of Saturn's teeth, she pried herself out of her mother's teeth, and with a wan smile assumed the Bhujangasana, the Cobra Pose. The hypothalamus, the metathalamus, white matter. A dark shadow fell over the station as the head of the future daughter, the head of a giant cobra, towered above.

"Why are we going there?" Běta asked, "Grandpa and Grandma died long ago."

"Is that any reason," her sister wondered, "not to go see

them? You really are weird," she kept shaking her head, "you were always weird."

The meninges.

Finally, one train stopped at the platform. A child's face appeared, pressed against the window of a compartment, and when his eyes met Běta's, he stuck out his tongue at her.

"Aren't we getting on?"

"No," Nadia said, "it's going either left or right. We're waiting for a different train."

"Namaste," Alice greeted the newcomers in Sanskrit, "please assume the Camel Pose."

The past and future had Běta in an icy grip, and in the station's restroom were pictures and writing she didn't understand. All of a sudden, she was no longer sitting with her sister in the waiting room nor waiting on the platform — this was Nadia's office in the Czech Museum of Music. The No. 12 tram passed by the window in the direction of Malá Strana Square, another toward Anděl. The windowpane gently rattled. The siren of an ambulance. Běta knew them well, they were always passing by her apartment building on the way to the Motol Hospital ER. She counted nine in total that night.

"How's Mom holding up?"

"Okay, I think. I went to sell something to an antiquarian and she told me to sell her instead, that she's the greatest antique of all."

Nadia laughed. "Will you come to the opening?"

Oh God. Hopefully it won't be *The Bartered Bride* again. Kecal takes Jeník aside and the drunkards begin to dance.

"The exhibition's called *Godmother Death*."

Běta must've heard wrong. "I'll come. For sure. And do you

remember how we once took the train by ourselves to go see Grandma and Grandpa?"

"Of course. We missed the train and were left stranded in that chilly waiting room for two hours."

"It wasn't chilly, there was that old Club."

"What?"

"A Club stove."

But Běta was no longer thinking of stoves or waiting rooms — express and local trains sped and rattled in all directions along the quadrillion synapses running between the nerve cells in her brain. Somewhere amid those endless connections was her daughter, in the Sarpasana, the Snake Pose.

She closed her eyes. Behind her eyelids a rather decrepit and rusted handcar was now going past on the other track with a cargo of words.

Good night, metaphors of mine,
in which I wished to capture time,
to let water flow. Will we ever notice
the shadow that's settled in my voice?

The Smíchov Synagogue

I set off for Anděl, this time on foot. Once again a bloom had coated everything for several days, a layer of frost, I had to resist it, not become resigned, not give up, I repeated Doctor Gnuj's words to myself, I needed to fight it with my breathing, to inhale all the way into the stomach and exhale warmth, my breath again and again, breathe out into the frost at least a small circle round like a puck, into the frost on the body of things and people, the circle that appears when a child breathes hard on a frozen windowpane to see what's on the other side.

I wondered why the locked cemetery in Košíře is called Malá Strana Cemetery. And why I have the same amygdala as reptiles. And why Alice once had gravel burst into laughter under her sandals. Some people I encountered were running with pedometers strapped to their hips, others zipped by with Nordic walking poles, and others used a long snorkel to inhale the air above the treetops. It was -3°C. I looked up at the sky. Cloudy, and a head spanning over Prague like an infinite umbrella obstructed my view of the sky. And what if nothing were beyond the window? What if looking through the small circle would offer only emptiness, identical to the frozen glass?

A deep breath into the stomach, a deep breath out. I walked to its rhythm, the rhythm of my own breathing, as if I weren't walking to Anděl but around the sacred mountain of Kailash. Yes: I should have been falling to my knees and getting back up again, lying down and standing up, standing up and lying down, the two paintings in the plastic bag were knocking against my thighs and made walking a chore.

The church on Košíře Square, then down Slávy Horníka Street, I avoided Plzeňská. I passed villas with silent gardens, mute greenhouses, slides warped by frost into question marks. Everything along the way was asking: how much longer, Běta? You may have brought yourself to walk today, carrying those stolen paintings, but what baggage will you prepare for tomorrow?

Villas to the left, villas to the right. Some rose above the stiffened past — always a reconstruction, never a reproduction — those on the right were built by the very hands of the future itself, absent scaffolding.

I found myself on Na Popelce Street. I walked aimlessly for

a while. At last, Bertramka. A double stairway like a helix, an enclosed balcony and a barn with a granary, a garden with no music. I opened the door to the synagogue at last. Vinyl records and books for 11 crowns each. The synagogue housed the secondhand bookshop where I sold the Boudník my parents had given me for my eighteenth birthday.

"Can I help you?"

God knows why my heart started pounding like in the elevator when I visited my mom in Motol Hospital.

"I just . . ." I stuttered, "I'll just have a look around."

But the elevator passed the third floor where I was supposed to get off and continued higher, and higher . . . I suddenly noticed that above each floor button was the name of a city instead of a number. Brussels, Vienna, Paris . . . And not just popular cities, the seventh floor, for instance, was the Greenland town of Nye-Sukkertoppen, and the eleventh . . .

I panicked. After all, I had to get to Majdalena, but no such button existed. I frantically pressed all of them at the same time, and then it happened — all at once I found myself in the bookshop in the synagogue at Anděl.

"But I can clearly see," the antiquarian said as he tore the first mask off his face, "that you've got something for me in that bag." My gaze flitted over the spines of the books, I didn't have the courage to look up. "So what treasures did you bring me this time?" He warbled the last two words rather than spoke them.

A mask beneath the mask, hardly a surprise. He took both scalps squeamishly between his index finger and thumb and briskly filed them under the letter P. The masks were wedged between Poe on one side and Karel Poláček on the other.

The door opened, and a woman I'd met above the Motol Cemetery stepped into the bookshop. She set her Nordic walking poles in the corner and started to browse through the records.

"Well come closer, to the counter," the antiquarian commanded.

I wanted to escape by elevator to Vienna, to Brussels even, but it was no longer here. I removed the gloves from my shaking hands. I pulled out the two paintings from my bag and placed them on the counter in front of the antiquarian. What will he think of them? It was just yesterday evening that I'd surgically removed the last layers.

"But . . . ," he demurred.

"Of course, it used to be a still life with a partridge, originally, then a double helix, and then . . . You have to admit that . . ."

"I'll take *Don Giovanni*," the woman said.

"Madame, not that record, it's cracked."

I could tell the antiquarian was starting to lose his head. Little wonder, after those scalps.

"I don't mind," the woman insisted, "it's still Mozart."

"What's your offer?" I attacked. The woman took the record and left.

"But," he protested, now desperately, "these paintings are completely blank!"

"Excuse me," I said, "but I don't see any signs stating you don't buy minimalism!"

"But these are just," his eyes flooded with tears, "just two empty squares."

The woman was back. "That's what I said." She'd forgotten her walking poles. The antiquarian no longer had anything to tear off. The emptiness that gaped from under his masks was the same as in the paintings.

I stepped out the shop to the front of the synagogue. I looked at the window display. *Requiem* for 11 crowns. Oh God, this was mine and Melda's Christ, sans the thieves. One of them must have brought it here.

February 6, 2015

I opened my journal, *Synapse*. Chickens spend their entire lives within the confines the size of a shoebox. Some even the size of a wine box. Míra and Bobeš looked over my shoulder at the page covered in writing.

President Zeman requested not to be served by disabled waiters in Kroměříž restaurant.

Woman who survived the siege of Leningrad dies after being arrested for stealing butter from supermarket.

Nineteen-year-old sniper Tatiana fighting with Russian separatists in Ukraine claims: "In 2026, Russia will be everywhere. All of Europe will be ruled by Russia. God is whatever you believe in."

"Draw us a gallows," Bobeš said and handed me a pencil.

On the 23rd of March, 1966,

I step onto the balcony and light a cigarette. A woman about my age is standing on the balcony opposite, lighting a cigarette. It's not clear which one of us is the reflection in the mirror and which is standing in front of it. But down in the courtyard below, deep under the surface of time, is another person amid the waves of children's cries.

"Newspaperrr!" Mom yells out. I stop jumping rope and run

up the stairs. We sit down at the kitchen table, me, Mom, and Nadia, and cut *Rudé právo*, the Communist Party's daily, into squares of toilet paper.

The Communist Party of Czechoslovakia delegation welcomed in Moscow.

A significant percentage of women active in the building of our socialist society.

A telegram from the Central Committee of the Communist Party of Czechoslovakia congratulating the Mongolian People's Party on its 45th anniversary.

Iron ore will no longer freeze over in freight cars.

I found the lost sun in the night: it was illuminating the empire of the dead.

Ballad of the back stairway

"You'll get your presents in the evening, right now it's too much chaos," Mom said and handed you a hundred crowns for your aunt.

I had to cut you down just above the ground again, Alice said into the phone, like that time in my dream when you had grown into the ground between the elm and willow, and I had to rid you of the curse of inertness so that you could begin your journey.

This time around you weren't scaring anyone off, your trunk turned into a torso and your branches into limbs. Today was your seventh birthday. It was also the day you were moving from Křížovnické Square to Zborovská Street. Your dad pushed a borrowed handcart loaded with books through Kampa, there and back. Every so often one of the books would fall off, and since he was so tired, he would just leave it lying there.

You decided to confide in your aunt, you couldn't bear to be alone with your secret any longer. You walked across Kampa, maybe you'd run into Dad, you walked along the river, the swans tightly winding their snow-white necks around you. The plane tree nodded its consent. You had to run up onto the bridge to check if Knight Bruncvík hadn't by chance already set out into the world to find a lion for his coat of arms. You knew that the golden sword he wields was just an imitation — the real one slumbered in the mountain. There he stood, overlooking the Vltava, with that familiar maiden face and in full armor, determined to wait eons for your future, so his sword could cleave it into years, months, and days.

You went up Vlašská Street to Jánský vršek.

"Auntie, I have to tell you something, but you gotta swear not to tell anyone."

"I cannot swear to anything, Bětuška, as it would anger our Lord. But I can promise."

Your heart left your body and pressed itself against the winding stairway. It was only much later that you found out it's all right this way, because the heart starts to beat precisely and regularly only several months before death.

"I climb rooftops."

Aunt Kozlová was stunned into silence.

"That's dangerous, Bětuška. Let's go to the Church of Our Lady Victorious and give Infant Jesus fifty crowns. Show reverence to Infant Jesus and you shall fare well in life."

A man was positioned on the stairs in front of the church. He was holding a harmonica in his hand but didn't dare play.

"If these were normal times, Bětuška, this man would be begging. Now it's not allowed. Come on, let's give him something." She opened the man's clenched fist and placed a five-crown coin next to the harmonica.

So this was how my secret ends, you thought bitterly. The man didn't even look surprised and just disappeared in the walls of the church.

You didn't like churches. You often dreamed that someone locked you in one with Jesus. He didn't care, he was entertained by the candles, blowing them out and then relighting them like your dumb classmate Vaněček, but you desperately wanted to go out into the light.

"Let us pray. Say a prayer, too." Aunt Kozlová knelt down next to the pew, closed her eyes, and her lips opened and closed a fraction as if she couldn't breathe; you, though, only knew *Now I lay me down to sleep, I pray the Lord my soul to keep,* and Auntie's mouth closed, leaving only the thin line of her lips, she was shrinking, vanishing, and evaporating in a haze of frankincense, you weren't interested in someone having it to keep, your soul, it belonged solely to you, you recognized only the angels you looked after, angels that die almost as soon as they're born, because they're made of water, angels with the outline of your body in the snow.

It lasted for ages, the praying, but you didn't have the courage to interrupt your aunt. You'd amuse yourself with Infant Jesus for the time being. A legend was written next to the statue. "The statue, originally from Spain, represents Jesus at a few years old, clothed in a long, flowing robe below which his tiny, bare feet are visible. According to legend, the Infant Jesus appeared miraculously to the monk who then modeled this statue out of wax based on his vision."

You thought the chubby kid in the manger looked hideous.

Good thing he's made out of wax, you thought, Infant Jesus could just be shoved into the oven.

Auntie finally got up. She looked at Infant Jesus and froze. At first you didn't understand why, its hideousness couldn't have shocked her like it did you, she'd been coming here and bribing him for years, and then, then you saw it: Infant Jesus's robe had turned blue and his peeping feet green. The color combination of dread. Your aunt clutched you as if you were a straw, a stem comforting in its whiteness, a stem from here to there, from blue and green into emptiness.

In the evening, you got some Play-Doh for your birthday along with a leather-bound notebook, one too fancy for your gallows. Kampa was asleep, strewn with your father's books. A nocturnal walker leafed through one of them: "Anything *even* never leads to good. Rhyme is something *tertiary*."

You worked the Play-Doh into a single greasy ball and flung it from the balcony into the courtyard. It never landed — instead, it rose gently above the rooftops into the night sky and joined the stars.

I was quietly dusting,

while Mom slept, those microscopic particles of mineral and organic origin. Mom slept, or her eyes may have just been closed, because suddenly, without having opened them, she said: "When I was fourteen, I fell in love with the son of the undertaker at the Jewish cemetery in Německý Brod. His name was Otík Pick. He was always carrying a bundle of stones on his back to get stronger. Josefína Procházková stole him away from me. I'll never forgive her for that. He died in Terezín, didn't even make it to Auschwitz."

I was afraid to speak to Mom. I carefully sat down on the side of the bed. Mom breathed out into the silence. It wasn't absolute — the ticking of Grandpa's clocks was coming from all sides, many of them unfortunately still worked. Maybe they were metronomes accusing me of constantly being out of step. I was about to scream. I could no longer bear it. Getting punched for the hayloft beam.

"I got my first kiss," Mom started talking again, "from Láďa Bezzemek. It tasted like cold fish. Brrr."

If those particles were also of organic origin, it followed that they were also part of my mother. I took a calculator and worked out that Mom got her first kiss seventy-six years ago.

"Borhyová keeps her baby attached to her breast!" Mom suddenly laughed in her sleep, "her husband beat her so badly her eye ruptured. Her vagina's made of pig intestines."

Of course. That morning she'd been browsing through the tabloid *Blesk*. "I see a great city," she suddenly prophesied, "whose demise will touch the depths."

"The depths?"

I glanced around. The Smíchov apartment had turned into a replica, a false imitation of some completely different project, into a panel from Nadia's exhibition on death. My duster was useless here.

Mom finally opened her eyes. "I had a dream."

On February 8, 2015, at one o'clock on the dot, a time-worn cuckoo bird shot out of the clock over Mom's head. "Dreams are pure nature," the cuckoo said, "the genuine truth." "No *quantité négligeable*," another added, "should they seem pointless to us, then it is we who are missing the point."

"I was in the river. In Německý Brod. I was sitting with my

mom on the weir, not a soul in sight, we were totally alone. We were laughing and peeing into the river. I knew that as long as we kept sitting there, Mom wouldn't die. Suddenly, I felt a force, a sinister force, behind me. I turned around to look: at first I thought it was an enormous wave, as tall as the plague column standing in the square in Brod, but it was something different altogether, something alive. Where am I? Mom isn't here with me. The maw of a sea monster had swallowed me whole and I found myself inside it. Furniture from my dollhouse was also inside this leviathan, but enlarged to leviathan proportions. There was even a piano. A grand piano. A tiny Mozart stood next to it, throwing a fit because he couldn't reach the keys. I didn't care. I wanted to get out and find my mom, what use was immortality to her on the weir if I wasn't with her. Bamboo holders were hanging throughout the bowels of the creature with the kind of newspapers gentlemen read at Hotel Slunce. I looked at a newspaper to find out what date it was, but it read 2300 BC. We were evidently floating somewhere, against the current of time. And then I woke up. I was standing over the grave of a saintly girl in the Malá Strana Cemetery in Košíře, the grave and entire cemetery were covered in ivy, and I suddenly realized that the saintly girl was my mother. And then I woke up again and —"

"Mom," I raised my voice, "but right now, you're actually awake, understand?" The flow could no longer be stopped.

"That cow Procházková, that traitor. I would always go to the Procházka family to get tutored in German. We were tutored by Fräulein Inge . . . The mother always gave us Pischingers, small, round wafer cakes, they were awfully tasty."

"You forgot something," I said, but Mom was already

breathing in and out steadily. "You forgot something," she parroted quietly, her lips barely moving.

"In those newspapers, in *The Czech Word* and *People's Justice* and *People's Gazette* and in *National Liberation*, in all the news articles, there was a small, round hole, just large enough for a snake to slip through from here to there, from the past into the future."

"Round . . . just large enough . . . snake," Mom smiled in her sleep.

"Yeah. As if a puck had flown right through those newspapers."

"A puck or — Pischinger."

Mom got her first kiss from Láďa Bezzemek on September 30, 1938. Our own allies — a gaping hole in the evening edition of *The Czech Word*, too — ordered us around like the vanquished.

It was three p.m. on the dot. The hatch on Grandpa's cuckoo clock opened a bit and I shot out, planed smooth by time.

The primer

Marta Semelová, Alice's teacher in first grade who so enthusiastically welcomed the death of Václav Havel in December 2011, presently a Communist MP, tried to cloak my daughter with the dictatorship of the proletariat. I swiftly leapt up and ripped it off like a scab.

Lillången

Nadia and I went to IKEA to pick out a new kitchen unit for the Smíchov apartment. It was snowing heavily. The pillow of a grayish sky smothered the parking lot. No shortcuts here, we had to follow the arrows and shuffle through all the departments. I tried not to look up, squinting my eyes and fixing my gaze on the shoes trudging along in front of me. I'd been here three times in total, with three of my partners, and it had culminated in a fight every single time. But Nadia rushed off happily into this living catalogue, caressing the pieces of furniture, disappearing in armchairs, and spinning around joyfully on office chairs. I decided to put a leash on her, and we shambled onward. A deep water moat surrounded IKEA, we were all stranded here. Nobody seemed to mind though. Children plunged their hands into bottomless boxes full of stuffed animals, and a couple was lying on one of the king-sized beds — she prayed, he thought about how he'd be assembling paradise back home guided by the instruction manual. Some customers couldn't help themselves in the bathroom department and sat on the toilets and lay in the bathtubs. Children screamed. Baby carriages ran over my toes. Nadia thrashed about on her lead. The torsos and skeletons of things stuck out of the racks in the warehouse section below us. My sister had obviously gone crazy and proceeded to throw anything that came her way into the shopping cart, an Åderblad curtain, a Stocksund three-seat sofa, a Notudden hanging storage organizer. I repeated the words to myself like incantations, but it was no help. For several days, frozen in satori, we decided between a Ringskär and a Ramsätra soap dispenser. The democratic design spired to the ceiling, it slipped out through openings into the heavy snowfall, into the parking lot, up to the sky, all this junk piled up and coalesced into a mountain, into a plague column, into the Tower of Babel looming over Prague, I wanted to be here, too, I wanted to be involved, to be a part of things and people — I had a go at creating my own bathroom style.

At the information desks, priests in yellow uniforms stood in front of their screens and gave counsel. Suddenly . . . but it couldn't be! Here! I suddenly thought I'd spotted Melda in the crowd. Stupid. Nothing was more absurd than a homeless person in an IKEA. And yet someone covered my eyes from behind as I stood in front of an Aläng floor lamp.

"Hey dere, Běda!"

"How much did you sell Jesus for, you Judas?"

We made ourselves comfortable in the Stockholm collection. I looked around but Nadia was nowhere to be seen. She had broken loose of her chain and disappeared.

"Where do you live now?" I asked, my gaze skimming over the passing shoppers with their loaded carts. "In the aviary?"

I must've really hit the nail on the head. Melda was completely plastered with black feathers like a raven puppet. He stayed silent for an unusually long time. The rustle of the masses swirling around us, along with the smell of meatballs — Swedish *köttbullar* — and wood.

"It's a secret, but I'll tell you, it being you and all." He lowered his voice, and I could hardly hear him. "Every day I wait here till nine when IKEA closes. Then I hide in one of the storage spaces in the bedroom department, and I come out when the coast is clear and it's all empty and quiet. At night I wander around a quiet IKEA that belongs to me alone. Let me tell ya, not even that billionaire Kellner has so much furniture. I lounge in the armchairs, sprawl out on the beds, I pretend to wash myself in the fancy bathrooms and to cook spaghetti in one of the kitchen units. I'm particularly fond of the Karensglatt. They open at nine a.m., and I just blend into the crowd and that's that. Been living here like this for a month now, it's like heaven."

When I closed my eyes, I could see the towering, swirling turret beneath my eyelids. I clambered to the top up the back stairway that coiled around it. I left the world of phenomena behind, colors and all. I finally managed to reach and stand in a spot above which was nothing. A Lillången wastebasket was perched by my feet. I turned my pockets inside out and tossed into it several hours, days, months, and years.

IKEA would be closing soon. Melda started to hobble toward the storage spaces. Everyone swarmed out, to the parking lot, with bags full of toothpicks so that they'd have something to pierce their hearts with that evening.

Petřín Hill

I walked through the Hunger Wall, also called the "Toothed Wall," and opened my journal *Synapse* in the Květnice Garden. I skipped the news. "Steel and marlstone, marlstone and steel. Observation tower made of steel, Hunger Wall made of marlstone. I've just passed through it and opened this journal in the Květnice Garden."

Even though I had that cadaverous look like in an ID photo, inside the Petřín Mirror Maze a grotesque grimace was reflected back at me. My mouth, agape like in Munch's painting, was so monstrously stretched that nothing was left of my face, just the tongue, teeth, and a gash of pink mucosa.

The tube of a telescope protruded from an opening in the Štefánik Observatory, a blue net full of loops was thrown over the sky. Even my lips formed a sort of loop, a loop through which my own time floated into my viscera, all those past years, months, days, and seconds. I ingested it all with ease, even the enormous fish that had swallowed Mom, the whale whose belly held the grand piano, the First Republic newspapers in bamboo holders, all of it.

Wanting to take the funicular, I blended into a cluster of tourists. I mixed in as they took photos so that I'd make it to faraway lands I'll never get to visit. Sometimes I wanted to be background, other times the dominant feature.

Next stop, Malá Strana Square. I repeat my mantra of all the stops on the No. 12 tram route. Mom is inside the fish, the fish is inside me, and my eyes have turned into two mirrors that grotesquely reflect reality, the reality of which only pink mucosa will remain, only to have my eyes abruptly turn into magnifying glasses — the small is large and the large is small — magnifying the seen to such a degree I'm unable to make out what it is I'm actually seeing, the leg of an insect, a skin pore, the fragment of a letter in Alice's email, or the Church of St. Nicholas.

I must be dreaming, because I clearly hear the name of the next stop: Nerja, Costa del Sol.

The No. 12 follows the curve of the bay and then runs along the coast, cliffs tower on the left while the rising tide laps at the tram's side from the right. I can smell the fierce, salty wind, the wind they call bora, which rushes through the windows and swirls inside the tram. Several passengers are engrossed in their phones, oblivious, just one child presses her awestruck face against the glass, floaties adorning her arms. I didn't pay the fare. Only now do I close my journal.

The beacon of a lighthouse revolves at the end of the pier, its light blinking. This time I'll be whole, I promise, Alice, whole and complete, not severed into two halves.

Three hounds spring toward me. "Mom . . ." I quickly take

the little backpack off your shoulders, the one I sent you to the orphanage with twenty years ago.

"Mom, I'm scared I won't ever see Grandma again."

"Don't worry," I say, and finally, on the seashore with Alice, I cease to be merely a scream. "I've brought her here. Grandma is inside a fish and the fish is now forever inside me."

February 19, 2015

Somewhere, in front of a shack, the air hovered thirstily and waited to become a word.

On the Senkaku Islands of Japan the wind mimicked the probable outline of an island.

In the Louvre, the Akkadian statue of Ebih-Il, which has no mouth, the statue of the first superintendent of the Mari city-state, turned slightly, pedestal and all, against the course of time.

Bonfire II

Everyone began to emerge out of the darkness and slowly approach the bonfire. Even Doctor Gnuj was here, scrunching in his pocket graphs mapping the occurrence of manic depressive disorder in Central Bohemia, patiently waiting for the fire to emit archetypes.

"I'm here," my sister Nadia said, agitated, "to get my exhibition materials back, my panels on death."

Mom in her adjustable bed lay under a rock overhang, and she was laughing as though she'd seen Otík Pick here, the flames blazing in her eyes. Bob Dylan stood by a pile of logs — he grabbed the tambourine and launched into an off-key rendition of the "Ode to Joy" while Míra and Bobeš rattled their mints to the beat. Melda's feathers got a bit singed.

I suddenly spotted Dad. He emerged from the darkness with his handcart full of books. At first I was alarmed that he was going to throw them into the flames, but he just reached into the fire as if it were totally normal and said, "don't worry, Běta, it doesn't take, it returns," and I could see how more and more books flew out of the flames into his arms, Proust's *In Search of Lost Time* and a chronicle of the Majdalena village dating back to 1894, and I even saw some sort of wooden skeleton extracting itself from the fire and now falling into a heap by my father's feet, it was his hayloft beam, and Alice said, "you couldn't walk, you were a tree, but I chopped you off just above the ground, at last you can walk, go in whichever direction you wish," and I listened to her and I left them all behind and I went into the darkness toward the cliffs.

I climbed over the rocks and found myself at Anděl. Just a couple stops by bus, Klamovka, Kavalírka, Kotlářka, and I'll be home. I took a deep breath of the air. It still smelled like the sea that had last been here in the Paleozoic Era.

NOTES

11   Nový prostor: Like other street papers, *Nový prostor* [New Space] employs the homeless and unemployed as vendors as a form of support. They can be seen hawking the magazine at most metro stations, such as Anděl in Prague 5.

16   *a Kladruber horse:* From the National Horse Breeding Farm in Kladruby nad Labem. Established by Emperor Rudolf II in 1579, the breed was used for royal and imperial occasions and to this day for state funerals.

16   *"Death is a mere part of hard life":* From Jiří Wolker's poem "Umírající" ["As I Lie Dying"] (1924).

19   *Landa or Gott:* Daniel Landa and Karel Gott, popular Czech singers. While Landa has been associated with the extreme right, Gott, perennial winner of the Czech Nightingale Award for best vocalist, is notorious for participating in the Communist regime's campaign against dissidents who signed Charter 77.

21   *"What is truly irrational . . .":* In Imre Kertész, *Kaddish for an Unborn Child*, trans. Tim Wilkinson (New York: Vintage, 2004).

25 *How to brave that moment . . . :* From "Psalm 34" by Ivan Diviš, in *Žalmy* [Psalms] (1986).

29 *Antiperle mints:* Akin to Tic Tacs, they came in a round plastic container and were commonly available during the communist era.

30 *ingenious concept, terrible execution:* From "Psalm 46" by Ivan Diviš.

30 *Vít Bárta:* Czech Minister of Transport accused of bribery in 2011 by members of his own political party, leading to his resignation from the government; some random guy popped up before the trial was to begin and requested to be a witness, which was refused.

39 *a stain upon a stain, a louse's louse . . . :* From "Psalm 4" by Ivan Diviš.

40 *"I'd just like to find . . .":* From "Psalm 41" by Ivan Diviš.

40 *"Nobody ever gets used to a constant feeling of injustice, . . .":* The opening lines of Vladimir Neff's novel *Sňatky z rozumu* [Marriages of Convenience] (1957).

53 *"The body, creaking in collapse . . .":* A paraphrase of "Psalm 46" by Ivan Diviš.

54 *an unfamiliar polyp floats through the room:* From "Psalm 47" by Ivan Diviš.

55 '. . . *oh, body, you beautiful dynamo, . . .*': From Josef Hora's poem "Zápisky z nemoci" [Diary of Disease] (1945).

56 *But all those years!:* From Josef Hora's poem "Popelka přebíra hrách" [Cinderella Picks Out Peas], in *Zahrada Popelčina*

[Cinderella's Garden] (1940). "All those bloodied growth rings! And seconds beyond count" is a paraphrase.

57 *everything that had ever existed was contained in that round light: words and days, the arm in a cast, and familiar faces,* . . . : A play on the line "everything that was passes by me in a ball of light: words, days, and heads . . ." from Josef Hora's "Cinderella Picks Out Peas."

57 O vain reason . . . : From the same poem by Josef Hora.

58 *Elms:* The first lines of this section are taken nearly verbatim from the Wikipedia entry.

58 *flint, bronze, and steel:* From Josef Hora's poem "Bojiště věčné" [Eternal Battlefields] (1936).

61 . . . yearning for the white, . . . maggots keep you company: From Josef Hora's "Cinderella Picks Out Peas."

63 . . . *to bear the mire of life like a rose:* From Josef Hora's "Cinderella Picks Out Peas."

63 *"I have to make it on my own . . .":* From a Karel Gott song.

64 *"The hard, green ice . . . and quietly finished his supper.":* From *Owl at Home* by Arnold Lobel (1975).

65 For ages I buried myself . . . : The first stanza of "Psalm 13" by Ivan Diviš.

65 *the sieve of the sifting pan:* From Josef Hora's "Cinderella Picks Out Peas."

71 As anger alone . . . : From the poem "Španělským dělníkům" [To the Spanish Workers] by Vladimír Holan (1937).

74   *A horizontal fall:* "Vivre est une chute horizontale," Jean Cocteau, *Opium* (1929).

76   *"that some energy impression is left . . .":* A paraphrase from *An Anthropologist on Mars* by Oliver Sacks (1995).

86   *Ryba's Christmas Mass chorale:* Jakub Jan Ryba (1765-1815) is known for composing *Czech Christmas Mass "Hey, Master!"*; *ryba* means "fish," thus the association in the next sentence.

87   Time, brother to my heart . . . : From the poem "Čas bratr mého srdce" [Time, Brother to My Heart] by Josef Hora (1927).

93   *"The same spot viewed . . .":* Quoted in *Cezanne*, by Ambroise Vollard, trans. Harold L. Van Dorfer (New York: Dover Publications, 1984) 74.

97   *Klamovka, Kavalírka, Kotlářka:* Three consecutive tram stops on Plzeňská Street, just past Anděl, in the Košíře district of Prague 5.

105   The psyche pre-existent to consciousness . . . : From C.G. Jung, "The Psychological Aspects of the Kore" (1951).

108   Godmother Death: The Czech equivalent of the Brothers Grimm's fairy tale "Godfather Death."

109   Good night metaphors of mine, . . . : A stanza from Josef Hora's poem "Zasněný vlak" [Train of Dreams] (1936).

111   *a garden with no music:* It is generally held that Mozart stayed at the Bertramka villa for a few months in 1787 to complete *Don Giovanni* and see it premiered in Prague's Estates Theater.

117   *Německý Brod:* The town was renamed Havlíčkův Brod in 1945.

118   "*I see a great city, . . .*": Legend has it that Princess Libuše, the mythical ancestor of the Přemyslid dynasty, had a vision of the city of Prague and uttered, "I see a great city whose glory will touch the stars."

120   *Our own allies:* The Munich Agreement was signed on September 30, 1938, in which Britain and France pressured Czechoslovakia to cede part of her territory, the Sudetenland, to Nazi Germany, eventually leading to the dismemberment of the country and the complete occupation of Bohemia and Moravia in March 1939 by Nazi Germany.

ZUZANA BRABCOVÁ (1959—2015) was born in Prague to the literary historians Jiří Brabec, a signatory of Charter 77, and Zina Trochová. Denied by the Communist regime the opportunity to study at university, she worked as a librarian, hospital attendant, and as a cleaning lady for six years. After the regime fell in 1989, she had a short stint at the Ministry of Interior before serving as an editor at Prague publishing houses. In her last years she was unemployed. Her first novel, *Far from the Tree*, came out abroad in samizdat in 1987, and for it she became the first recipient of the Jiří Orten Prize. The novel was officially published in Prague soon after the Velvet Revolution. She published two more novels over the next decade before taking a twelve-year break. In 2012, her novel *Ceilings* was published, which brought her a Magnesia Litera Award for Prose Book of the Year, and this was followed by *Aviaries* in 2016, completed just before her unexpected death.

TEREZA NOVICKÁ was born in California to Czech parents who had fled Communist Czechoslovakia. She grew up in San Francisco before moving to the Czech Republic in 2000 and completing her BA in English and MA in American Literature at Charles University in Prague. She has translated a number of Czech and Slovak poets into English, including Ondřej Buddeus, Jan Těsnohlídek, Nóra Ružičková, Ondřej Škrabal, Sylva Fischerová, Lenka Daňhelová, Olga Pek, and Jan Škob. She is the co-translator of Vítězslav Nezval's *The Absolute Gravedigger* and the forthcoming *Woman in the Plural*.

AVIARIES

Zuzana Brabcová

Translated by Tereza Novická from the Czech *Voliéry*,
originally published in 2016 by Druhé Město, Brno

Design by Silk Mountain
Set in Janson Pro and Univers
Frontispiece by Rybka
Cover by Dan Mayer

First Edition 2019

TWISTED SPOON PRESS
P.O. Box 21 — Preslova 12
150 00 Prague 5, Czech Republic
twistedspoonpress@gmail.com
www.twistedspoon.com

Printed and bound in the Czech Republic by PB Tisk

Distributed to the trade by

SCB DISTRIBUTORS
www.scbdistributors.com

CENTRAL BOOKS
www.centralbooks.com

The publisher extends his gratitude to
Edgar de Bruin of Agency Pluh and the
Ministry of Culture of the Czech Republic
for their continued cooperation and support.